I0772590

Wonder

A New Testament

Published 2024 by Britton Speaks LLC

III

Acknowledgements

To Vicky for nursing my soul back to health and raising the bar for friendship. Thank you for sharing your goodness, beauty and honesty with me over and over again. Thank you for the years of friendship in spite of the miles that have often existed between us. You have been the friend, the sister and the cheerleader that energized me to complete this book. Thank you for sharing your divine riches and thank you for allowing us all to live under your sky. You are the breath of God.

To Marzena for the love and support you have shown me in my most trying times. Who knew such a beautiful friendship could be formed over tea and toast morning after morning? Although we started as roommates, I am grateful to call myself your brother. I have a renewed sense of love, family and good bread thanks to you. Your love and care helped to walk me down the final stages of getting this book to the world. I am forever grateful for the family we have in each other. You are sunshine wrapped in chocolate.

To Scott for providing the perfect watering of peace, love and encouragement so that I could focus on my art. I am forever grateful for how you have loved and held me since day one. Your love and support have not gone unnoticed… What would I have done without your pats on the back? Glad I will never know. You are a splashing river of love.

To Danny for loving me through thick and thin. You have loved me in a way that is both palpable and intangible. I am grateful to have had a front row seat to your blossoming and looking forward to what life has in store for you. You are a royal blessing.

To Morea for being present in your absence, for being there when you're not. Thank you for teaching me the insignificance of distance and the richness of time. Our relationship has taught me that to be seen and heard has nothing to do with physical proximity. What a pen pal you've been, or dare I say voice pal? You are a warm hug on a snowy day.

To Alystra for showing up. I don't know where you came from, but I am so glad you did. Seemingly out of nowhere, you held me with your magic and lifted me with your love. You are more than a friend, you are an angel sent from above.

To Arcelious for your there-ness. The love, support and wisdom you've shared over the years have helped me to put one foot in front of the other when I couldn't see my feet. You are the reason I dance with the wind.

To the Pink Lady for being more than just the spark of inspiration for this book. Thank you for being the evidence that LOVE is real and that LOVE is life. May your marvelously loving spirit forever shower this world with grace. You forever live in my heart and remain an eternal part of my soul. You are infinitely wondrous.

Author's Preface

That thing that rises then recedes, rocks then jolts, electrifies then propels, I have been taught to call "love". At other times, "amor", and quite often, "Liebe". Three simple words that supposedly describe or identify the swelling I feel within. But what happens when you awaken to recognize that the languages you've been given don't equate nor give justice to that thing you feel pulsing and swaying inside? What does one do when those words fail to reflect the magnitude of waves crashing and rising inside?

Was there ever a time in our collective history when that sea of beautifully articulated emotions could adequately be described and contained within a little bitty word such as love? Can this thing be compressed into a simple sound, a 1 or 2-syllable word, that rolls from the tips of our tongues? Is it quantifiable? After all, how much gold is a unit of love even worth?

Like the ocean, can it ever be portrayed in its entirety without mention of what lies beneath? Do we do the oceans any justice when we mention their splendor and might without mention of the great whales, starfish and layers of corral beneath? And within that logic, do we do justice to that tremendous collection of things we feel inside, if we never mention its cooperative and defining components?

Who among us views that richness that surges in a moment as one singular thing? Is the word love somehow shorthand to describe the thrust I feel that can only, at best, be portrayed as a place written in fairytales, seen in dreams, and felt in a beat? Does it represent an ecosystem that responds to the gravitational pull of the moon, while simultaneously being gracious enough to faithfully make way for me whenever I choose to dive in? No matter the size nor significance of any body of water - whether it be in a storm or the stillness of night - does water joy and laugh when I splash, sip, and sneeze?

How do we understand the basic properties of water, without first writing a dissertation about what it does for and to a child on a hot summer's day? What does water do to the child that treats the wet substance as more than a simple quencher of thirst or carrier of ships, but rather, an over-abundant resource meant to be played with and splashed around?

How is it that when you put children together with something as simple as a garden hose, it is always a recipe for piercing shrieks that penetrate the hearts and minds of anyone in earshot of the childish excitement?

If you ask me 'what is water', all I can say is that it's a representation of the expansive seas, cannonballs with my brother and sister of decades past, and the ways children use it to explore, make the day brighter, funnier and more adventurous.

However, if you ask me 'what is love', I pause…

Then I think. I cry, I sob, I laugh, I jump for joy. And still, I Wonder.

Is love meant to describe the smallest basic unit of a phenomena or event that we feel emotionally? Or is love analogous to a drop of water? Or is love meant to describe an ever moving and cycling ecosystem of events and happenings that is analogous to the depths of the ocean? Or do we simply need a better word to describe what happens to me every time I am lucky enough to be visited by another hummingbird, see a yellow flower, feel the sun's warmth upon my skin, view the world from yet another mountaintop and bury my toes in the sand while staring out at the moon?

What do we call it?

What should I call it?

Or better yet, what do we call that thing that is sensed at our most enchanting moments?

This book is meant to provide new language for a word that has lost its meaning, or perhaps has expanded beyond its original usage. We have reached a place in society where the word love can be used by someone who isn't being loving, but at the same time love can be meant sincerely and somehow it isn't sensed nor received. This book serves as a remedy to expand our concepts of love, or whatever you wish to call it. This is my humble attempt to recontextualize what it means to love and broaden our ability to love each other and everything around us unreservedly and unflinchingly.

Is this a religion, you ask?
To that, I must wholeheartedly declare that it is one of the best. Furthermore, this book is far more likely to unravel or poke holes in whatever religions you may be carrying, rather than convert you. On other occasions, it may strengthen your religious convictions and thereby cause you to love more expansively... Either of which make me smile.

Is this a dogma?
Don't be silly nor closed minded.

This entire book was written from a place so deep within my being, although its source feels more distant than that of our neighboring galaxies, while also feeling nearer than the pages my pen massages.

This book was born out of my lifelong endeavor to understand how the world inside of me impacts the physical world I see with my eyes and vice versa. In order to produce this material, I had to toss aside many beliefs handed to me and - at times - forced upon me, to uncover a deeper underlying truth or truths. The kind of truth so real, so vibrant, so healing that it cannot be denied and requires no scientific, societal, religious nor political approval.

This text also describes a godthing, not as a futile attempt to prove that there is or isn't a god. Nor is it a silly attempt to prove that god is real or isn't. I am not foolish enough to debate such piddly notions. However, what cannot be denied is that it is a continual concept that our species won't stop pondering nor questioning. Find that fucking gene! Or maybe it's an enzyme, a cell, or an organ nudging us all to come up with a fucking consensus. The goal of the species is not to debate it, but rather, to create it. Create a godthing together so profound and wonderful, and for EVERYONE. Create something so loving and freeing that we all can at least say in laughing jest "if there were a wondrous godthing out there, this should be it!" It will unite us all. Mark my words!

From an early age, individuals have shoved their religions into my face. I've seen and heard of religious perspectives that condone state executions and gunfire upon the land I currently stand and beyond. None of which have ever made any sense to someone like myself who seeks to understand love, warmth, joy and the value of life.

As a child, I was told stories about a god that had the character of someone I wouldn't let into my house nor invite to coffee. A punishment-focused god seemed small and insignificant to my childish mind, and of course, to my 40-year-old psyche as well. Why would a godthing need punishment as a means to show its power and might? Moreover, individuals, societies and religious perspectives that prefer to punish rather than provide loving tools that allow for growth and expansion have always felt petty, looked backward, and smelled fishy.

Since I was five years old, every time someone made mention of a god, I always felt that I could create a better one. One that is more loving and accepts all parts of my being, not asking me to change, but simply to grow… Evolve.

Therefore, if you ask what genre I am writing, I call it *Philosophical Fantasy*. In other words: GOD creation. A practice that feels just as ancient as it does modern. The contents of my penmanship are drawn from an invisible source that even I have trouble pinpointing or naming.

In my opinion, if we are going to have a god to debate, believe in or deny, can we at least do it justice by creating one that is better, more loving and dedicated to our individual and unalienable right to Wonder, laugh, roam freely throughout the earth and show up in whatever identity we so choose? Rather than unquestioningly hold onto dusty or obsolete versions of god that have been handed down by our foremothers and forefathers.

The godthing depicted within this text counts no sins, condones no people cages, nor does it place power in the hands of those with the most destructive weaponry, nor in the hands of those with the biggest armies.

X

I woke up that fateful day with the realization that the greatest and grandest godthing I will ever know or hear of will have to be the one my pen creates. So I started writing, in hopes that I could share it with the world and encourage others to do the same. If your godthing is grand enough to love and include me as I am and wish to be, then we can be friends. Otherwise, please stand back and leave me alone forevermore.

Now, I must admit that calling my creation a god would be too small a term, concept, noun, or notion. Particularly given how the term is often flung about within the English language. You are already forgiven, prisons obsolete, governments petty and fizards weak. You are granted all of the lovely things you've ever desired and wished for that expands freedom, love and fulfillment for yourself and everyone in the great wide world around you.

These wishes are always granted first, keep that in mind as you wish, dream and fantasize away… Fantasize a bit further… Fantasize my dear. For this godthing pales all prior as well as future godlings, irrespective of religious or national affiliations. All are encouraged to be themselves and cultural norms constantly questioned. I offer Zeraww, synonymous with both Wonder and Aww and expressed with Love.

XII

"If we needed a reason to look up,

would stars sparkle, moons glow,

and birds fly?"

~ *Britton Lee*

Table of Contents

Walking in Faith

None of our worldly scholars know this, but the notion of god as the noun and or collection of nouns came about for one reason and one reason only. To get us to raise our hands and lift our eyes.

Far back in the endless beginning of our kind, the earliest elders of the tribe from which we all stem, pondered something about our common forms. Our bodies. That we had the collective ability to walk on two feet, so why were we all still crawling?

What started as a simple question became a simple wave that led to a simple landscape changing tsunami. Tsunami.

"Why are we all still crawling?" was the question that led our species into an endless series of psychological and spiritual pivots only to be described as the first waterless tsunami. Translated in today's terms within this context, would mean enlightened Wonder.

The yearning in the question produced our first shared goal as an entire planetary species. Going to the moon as a notion or an act is nothing in comparison to what we all accomplished together from that imaginative thrust.

Like dominoes falling in every direction, the species had reached a shared thriving that complemented our individual longings. Everyone was eventually hit by the wave of Wonder.

Furthermore, the question exuded an unspoken understanding that once my neighbor walks, we all begin to walk. Albeit, there were small factions in the beginning that resisted the enlightened Wonder because they were too reliant upon that which we now call evidence. Even in those days, not everyone could understand that physical evidence, itself, is a jokester. It can only whisper foggy insights into the past while saying very little about the future.

If evidence were a person, it would always be looking back, not knowing it could be looking forward and imagining deeper. Which can best be described as monoperspective. However, it didn't take long for the monoperspective faction of the tribe to believe in new possibilities for themselves and the world around them. It was bound to happen, as the god of monoperspectivism is a selfish god that serves no one and obscures beauty.

Meanwhile, our ancestral elders began to proclaim that we are all born just as much to crawl as we are to take a step. But knowing the poor physical balance that existed within the crawling species, the elders sat in meditation asking, "how are we going to achieve this feat?" While many may tire from constant questioning, the wise know that the god of questions is also the god of answers.

That's when it dawned on the elders all at once! Some say the moment was met with a flash in the sky, a rumble in the earth, and a burst of love so warm that the entire tribe let out a simultaneous breath that sounded like "Aww."

That my friend is the real Big Bang! The bang that revealed to us that all we had to do was encourage each other to lift our eyes and reach for the sky, thus intuitively activating the muscles of our legs and thus lead us closer to the clouds.

The elders scrambled to determine how to unfold the plan. You see, they had calculated that if we could first balance and strengthen our ability to reach for and look up at the sky for more than just food, we could eventually engage our legs in such a way that we could become trees. Standing balanced and erect. From there, the elders figured they could more easily work out how to walk. How to take that first step.

It was going to take what we now know as exercise to make this happen, therefore the elders realized it was time to create a god to keep our focus on the shared goal of walking.

Hoorah was its name and all it desired was praise and in return it would ensure that blue skies always reappear, yellow flowers always bloom, and rainfall every time you are desperate for it. And of course, with faith coupled alongside praise, the gift of walking would be bestowed upon all who joyfully and playfully praised Hoorah.

Praising Hoorah involved lifting one's eyes, then arms with a sincere belief that you could reach the clouds on the way to the stars.

The only commandment: praise Hoorah every time beauty is felt, seen, heard, or sensed.

Given the immense beauty all around, it took less than a full cycle around the fireball in the sky before we were all standing tall as trees. The entire tribe was actively praising Hoorah, which strengthened the muscles required for balancing on two hind legs.

Remarkable, yes. Surprising, no.

Along the way, as we noticed the progress amongst the species, our language began to change. Regardless of one's individual progress, we began to greet each other with the most overused yet underused phrase our species has ever known. "Keep reaching, you're almost there."

Keep reaching, you're almost there although started as a type of divine encouragement, became the way we said hello, goodbye and I love you.

It was our first shared prayer: "May we keep reaching, we're almost there" then we would all agree by letting out an "Aww" in unison.

The wisest elder of them all was asked by countless elders, "how do you know this plan will work?" And every time like all other times, that wisest elder replied by saying "I don't know, but it will."

"I don't know, but it will" was the only way to say "I know, because I have faith" in our ancestral tongue.

After many moons, it became evident that the entire tribe could stand balanced on two feet. That was the day the elders instructed the tribe to meet at the river to unveil the next steps of their plans. We, our ancestors, all standing as trees as if we were at the starting line of a race. The plan: take our first step. The stillness that existed on that windy day revealed that this was the day!

Waiting for the call at the starting line, a child blessed with a naivety so profound, one can only call it divine insight, or simply just call it Aww.

The youngster shrieked and began to sprint. The child ran as the entire tribe watched in complete and utter amazement. Like dominoes one after the other began to sprint, darting around like kids playing tag. Aimless, yet destined.

We as a species all ran before we could walk.

Remarkable, yes. Surprising, no.

Now, we've all heard that you must crawl before you can walk, but our souls know that we must lift our eyes before we can fly.

And so I say all that just to say… It's time for a new god, the god of flight. For when you fly, we all begin to fly. And that is how you say *I love you.*

Saying I Love You

whenever
time and space
bring us together
I am home
Is the meaning of Love

Starfish Clouds

If you have a leaf, is it a plant? Can twigs and branches be considered trees? Does a tree exist in its entirety if not considered nor drawn without its roots?

When does a rock become a pebble and a boulder a mountain? Is the carcass of a starfish a starfish? When is a starfish a starfish? Hmmm

Don't ask me, ask the rocks! But be patient as you await their response. They're asleep longer than they stir. Existing, pondering, dreaming, and questioning somewhere between the unseen inside and the seen outside.

Just as we may wonder if we are on the inside of something dreamt or the outside of something hoped, the rocks, mountains, meteors, and moons wonder too.

This story starts at the endless beginning of this place often called earth. That is to say, the planet we call home, preceding the advent of time. All that we see was formed from the somethingness of the nothingness. As it faded playfully in and out of physical existence. Thus existing nonexistently until delightfully complex molecular bonds were established, then solid matter began to form into a variety of semi-permanent and semi-impermanent structures. Forming what the wise and devine stars above refer to as Diaria, meaning: the region that blooms impossible outcomes and one day shall shine the brightest. But we foolishly call her Earth and bravely call her Mother.

Far into the endless past of Diaria, was the slow crystallization of our current physical home. This story goes back long before we used language to create lines between that which we call "living" and that which we call "dead" or "not alive". Long before anything wiggled, crawled, swam, or danced, there was a large solid mass submerged in the oceans of the area. The mass began to stir, wondering "what am I?"

Initially sounding no louder than a repeating thought in one's head. Like a neverending echo, the mass continued to ask…

"What am I?
    …what am I?
        …what am I?
            …what am I?
                …what am I?"

A millenia later, the question became an almost audible whisper, then somehow growing into a rumble on the deep sea floor where the mass rested. The rumbling intensified until it caused the earth to quake.

Building intensity and a sense of desperation to know the answer to its first question, caused the solid mass to splinter. The fracture grew until a small piece of itself broke off.

The shock of the event awakened the large solid mass and its fraction. Seeing itself for the first time, it recognized the fragment as a stone. Thus making the large solid mass, presumably, a rock, or perhaps a boulder. The boulder proclaims to the fragment, "although you are a fraction of me, don't forget that you are as much of a stone as you are a boulder."

The fragment, born from a question, laughed at the boulder replying with insights beyond its years. "I know the history of my body, but I also know that I'm a starfish, " said the fragment.

Laughing back, the boulder responded firmly, "there is no such a thing, this is clearly the land of water and boulders. "

The rocks slept another millennia before the large boulder turned back to the fragment and said, "you're still a rock my son."

"I've told you once before, I'm a starfish and clearly the first," the fragment replied with enough intensity to crack ever so slightly. The large boulder then proceeds to sleep, not as long as one might expect. But upon stirring the boulder awakens to see that the fragment had changed form. Now resembling the shape of a sparkle, as if plucked from the midnight sky.

Amused, the large boulder says "I see you've somehow changed shape, but you're still no starfish. All I see is a prettier stone before me, my son."

"I am a starfish" said the prettier fragment with a yearning strong enough to rattle its internal molecular structures, triggering a before-unlikely series of molecular events that appeared synchronized, intentional, and chaotic.

There was an uncountable number of moons before the big boulder stirred again. Awakened by a flurry of activity upon its surface. Feeling tickled, the big boulder recognizes it was now covered by slow moving creatures. "Who are you creatures smothering me, and where is my son, the pretty fragment I once called a stone?" the big boulder demanded to know.

One of the slow moving creatures responds with an air of accomplishment. "Father, it's a shame you do not recognize your only begotten son and my colony of sons and great grandsons"

Feeling baffled and confused, the big boulder angrily rumbles, producing magnificent waves at the water's surface. Thus creating the first oceanic tsunami.

"Son, you went from a stone to a starfish, to a colony of starfish. How did you do it? "Asked the big boulder.

"I don't know, but I did. I suspect my fantasies had something to do with it," replied the first ever starfish.

Being formed from a massive rock is not the most noteworthy part of the starfish story, as many creatures on our planet were initially formed from rocks. But starfish are one of the only earthly species whose entire population identifies as male. Before there was a flaming homosexual, there have been colonies of male gendered starfish. That's why they all gather around to love and caress each other like a collection of loving aroused men in holy fellowship when it's mating season.

It is irrelevant whether a starfish thrusts a cloud of eggs or a cloud of sperm into the sea. Take note, they all ejaculate at the height of their arousal.

Thus revealing that true masculinity has the faith of a rock with the loving ease and safety of a starfish.

And I say all that just to say… If a broken fragment can transform itself, so can you. And that is how you say *I love you.*

I Am Not a Human

Some call it Adam, some call it Eve. Truth is, that being wasn't called a human at all back then. Why? Because there were no words existing at that time, because our common ancestor had yet to form a grammatical language in the earliest days of existence. Lacking language as we know it, they had no words to label each other. There was, however, a sound for it. Sounded like "hooh-haata." It was the sound they made to call each other. In a similar fashion that a mother lion calls her cubs. Her cubs all respond to that one sound, as if they all had the same name.

"Hoohaata" was, in fact, the only sound they uttered from their lips. Birds chirp, dogs bark, cats meow, and cows moo. It was that sorta thing. Now, excuse my prying open of the English language, but back then the Hoohaata hoohaated. That was the beginnings of language as we know it and it predates hand and arm gestures as forms of communication.

The Hoohaata eventually learned to convey a small range of emotions by varying their tone when they hoohaated. Within a few generations, the clan had developed a fairly complex ability to communicate by alternating and patterning the sounds they used to convey emotions. Love, joy, bliss and wonder were the only emotions the Hoohata could express and therefore, say. For example, to communicate love, hoohaata was pronounced with a high pitch. On the other hand, Wonder was pronounced with the lowest.

This may be difficult to understand if you consider yourself to be a mere human, but back then, they had a culture too. Albeit primitive. Although, I've always assumed the meaning of primitive to mean: having THE primary mind. That is to say, the first thought, but more specifically, THE first consciousness. Our earliest ancestors possessed the consciousness of the energy that created the physical world without any separation.

Fear is an impossible emotion to experience when you are in touch with THE first consciousness. Needless to say, the fear of death had yet to enter the minds and culture of our hoohaata-ing ancestors. For fearing death is like fearing that you're late: a social construct improperly given access to the nerves in your brain that were solely meant to warn you of clear and present danger, such as a [1]"lion, tiger, or bear".

Late or not, you still exist. Dead or not, the same. What's to fear?

Fearing death is not the same as the fright one may feel when they are close to drowning. For that is a built-in survival mechanism to keep the organism alive. Similar to the "fight or flight" reflex we've heard so much about. Therefore, when one is close to drowning, it is not a fear at all. But rather, an intense hunger and reaching for life. Many of us have been hungry before, and many others know the pain of starvation. The hunger pains that the body manufactures serve as a reminder that it is time to locate food, which is triggered deep within the soul of the gut.

Drowning on the other hand, causes a lifehunger pain so intense that it becomes all you think about as you reach for, and grasp at - in sole

---

[1] "Lions, tigers and bears" is a reference to the line made famous by the character Dorthy, played by Judy Garland, in Wizard of Oz. A film released in 1939

pursuit of - the sweet sensations of life. It's neither a running away from nor an avoidance of death. It's a running into life.

I had never felt that desperate for anything. MY LIFE. I learned that nothing was more valuable than that very experience. A feeling I like to carry around even when I'm not drowning. Though I must admit, this is the same feeling I had when I was thrusted from the womb kicking and screaming. It is the same fucking feeling... Don't you remember?

The emotion is a cross between a roaring "I swear to god!" and a sexual yearning for pleasure.

I digress... The discussion was on the Hoohaata whose culture did not teach them to fear social constructs such as fear of one's government, debt, or not getting the promotion. Lacking fear, the overarching and predominant emotions of love, joy, bliss and Wonder were given expanded meanings as our language developed further.

The Hoohaata's language eventually involved a sequence of emotions to identify directions using references more often in the sky than land. For example: The sequence of emotions used to identify a direction could be Wonder, Wonder, love and the opposite direction would be stated in the reverse: love, Wonder, Wonder. There were no grammatical tenses at the time, however every thought and emotion was primarily forward thinking. That is to say, all communication was assumed to be about moving into the present moment. The expression of joy followed immediately by Wonder indicated a food or water source. Our early ancestors hadn't a need to differentiate between food and water in the first 100,000 years of our linguistic development, for it was all considered sustenance.

Language progressed rapidly as the common desire to communicate with each other grew, so did the corresponding regions of the brain as our species continued along its evolutionary path. Our common ancestors desired for a greater means of communication because they all had a single question they desperately needed to ask their fellow Hoohata.

Unbeknownst to each other, they all had the same question vibrating within their spirits long before there were words to express it. The very question that every society and civilization must grapple with.

While it is the individual's job to ask oneself "who am I" then proclaim it. It is the job of the collective to ask "who are we?"

These questions can be lovingly answered in just a moment, or we can all wait another 60 bobillionfahfillion fucking years.

And I say all that just to say… Our ancestors' desire to communicate drove the direction of their evolution. What will your desires do? And that is how you say *I love you*.

I Love You Means

Thank you
For creating a moment
I will not forget
Nor will I try

Nonexistent Fearlessness

y little nephew, Troy, loves the deep end of the pool, although he hasn't yet worked out the mechanics of swimming. And even worse, he prides himself on how long he can hold his breath. Scares me half to death. My poor heart can hardly take it.

I became a hero 695 times in just one weekend at the pool. We were constantly reaching out to keep him from drowning. But he couldn't see his limitations in spite of my efforts to expose them. So it had me thinking, do our limitations somehow disappear once we begin to disregard their presence? All the while, he's still jumping into the deep end. Why was he doing this? After jump number 622, it became clear to me. That he kept jumping into the pool, not because he was fearless and not because he felt any safety in our watchful hands. But rather, he jumped in the pool because he knew he could not drown. That is called faith.

When I think of our ancestors on those ships way back when. And then I think about the ones who said to themselves "AIN'T NO WAY IN HELL!" Ain't no way in hell has been said by our ancestors throughout our journey into the present. And those who said it, jumped from those ships, supposedly to die in the sea. But I don't believe we've ever been told the rest of the story. How did the story continue?

You see… In my dreams, and in my fantasies, and in the stories whispered long long ago, they knew - beyond a shadow of a doubt -

that they COULD NOT DROWN. "AIN'T NO WAY IN HELL!" They knew they had the knowledge to create new communities and civilizations deep below the sea where love, support, health and abundance would not only abound, but far exceed and surpass any supposed fantasy that they ever tried to sell us.

And so, I'm saying all that just to say... I hope you spend some time in the deep end and I wish you the faith of my little nephew Troy and our Ancestors to know that you cannot drown. And that is how you say *I love you*.

Happy Birthday to Us

How can it be that someone, something or some stories can get planted into your head without your permission, consent and or notice? It acts like a seed and on some occasions appears as a weed. While others can fester like a puss filled sore with a slow moving drip that dries up and crusts over before it ever has the chance to drip onto the freshly mopped floors.

These ideas, hopes and dreams grow like trees and branches into more wishes, drives and fantasies. That is, if you're not careful. Don't take what doesn't belong to you is how I was raised.

The world we live in makes it easy to proclaim the "safe" or "most logical" path or opportunity as your target, endpoint or goal. But when I stop to think about what pushes me inside or what drives my inner self, my goals and dreams begin to change. Because the original ones never belonged to me in the first place.

I knew this as I stirred, tossed and turned, up all night, reaching and grabbing, twisting and turning in the womb. Wanna know why that baby is twistin' and turnin' energized by the very love it assumes is out there waiting for it, without ever having seen it? Wanna know why that baby seems to be tap dancin' while reachin' for the stars? Ask my grandma.

Wanna know why that baby ain't moved in so long? Huh? How would you sleep after dancing for days while getting set to pick and choose which dreams you will use to spread love and joy throughout the land?

I remember!!!

I tend to ask my friends questions about their childhood. They don't know this, but I'm digging to uncover, discover, endeavor to find out if they remember too. It can make you go crazy when you know you remember something but so many don't seem to have a clue. It's not a matter of putting words to it, it's not a matter of being able to draw it, it's not a matter of finding the right language to describe it. You don't get to that memory by a boat or a train, "it's somewhere beyond the moon and the rain" as [2]Dorothy so beautifully reminded us. You just get there!

I remember those days as a seedling, I remember it well. Doesn't mean I haven't had moments where or when I forgot it between the glimpses of my days and between the glimpses of my nights. But like the lens of a camera and the passing of clouds, it always finds a way of coming back into focus.

And that is when I am reminded of which goals are mine to claim and which ones don't belong to me.

I haven't forgotten those budding moments. I remember that joyful darkness of the womb and the questions that arose from within. The first question that branched into a series of questions and answers one after another. Ultimately signaling my purpose. That first question was my very first thought.

---

[2] "It's somewhere beyond the moon and the rain" is a reference to the line made famous by the character Dorthy, played by Judy Garland, in Wizard of Oz. A film released in 1939

The first thought that formed as the sperm met the egg was so clear and loud that the sound of it still vibrates within my cells, and on occasion, rumbles through the sound of my voice.

That first thought... That first question created an intensity so great, it was akin to the Big Bang. Tremendous, effortless, momentous. Creating a heat so great it can only be described as loving unbridled excitement.

That warm loving excitement produced the momentum necessary for my single cell - albeit formed by two coming together - to split, divide and grow bit by bit. And with each newly multiplied cell, the question was answered. The initial answers were vague, then became increasingly more specific and simplified as the cells divided further.

You know, upside down doesn't it feel like upside down when you're hugged by the womb. For every perspective offers insights and the ability to answer that question. The great inevitable, and inescapable question.

I consulted with each and every star, learned from each and every planet, observed the physics and social order of galaxies. I conversed with my ancestors who had elevated to celestial beings, no longer residing in physical worlds as we know it. They told me their stories and I told them mine. As with every time before, they packed my bags for this journey called life. Its contents filled with morsels of wisdom, growing knowledge, deep insights, endless riches and a kind of sight only given to jellyfish, starfish, trees, mountain tops and moons.

My celestial ancestors equipped me with an amphibious nature. The ability to exist in multiple worlds as who I am. Like a tree that has one expression in air and another in earth. To the sub earthly creatures, the tree often appears as a collection of roots. To the birds, it appears as a woody stalk adorned with leaves that change with the seasons. But when you've had the opportunity as I have to exist as a tree, you know that the tree would never limit itself by calling itself a tree. For when the tree thinks and feels itself, it somehow knows who and what it is.

As a tree, there is never a moment when or where, that causes you to forget who you are. It is eternally and infinitely aware of this most simple and humbling of facts. For the tree knows and sees itself as a peacefully strong expression of love. The ants see it when they gaze upon the tree and so do the birds.

So, as I squirmed, danced and hummed in the womb, the question was repeated at every phase of my fetal development. The great and powerful question. That moves mountains, changes the tides, calls on storms and delivers refreshing rains that urge new life to grow.

The question keeps me up at night in absolute Aww. The question dictates my steps, it opens doors and frames conversations.

The question, if it hasn't dawned on you by now. The question that you may have forgotten will and forever will be the same.

And that is… how will I do it this time?

How will I be an expression of love and joy this time?

How will I be an expression of harmony and symbiosis in any world I find myself?

How will I make my expression of love and harmony, not simply amphibious, but also ubiquitous?

How will I do it this time and which tools will I use?

And I say all that just to say… Remember the question and you'll know who you are. And that is how you say *I love you.*

How will I do it this time and which tools will I use?

Imposter Syndrome

No one ever tells you that you can be really good at something you hate doing. But I somehow always knew. However, I rarely noticed the occasions when the practice defined me. Or at least, I allowed it to.

I used to be so good at things I hated. I'm not just talking about mopping the floor so well that it shines a whole week. I'm not just talking about American history as it's taught in schools, although it did help me to develop an important skill. That is to know something so well, and at the same time, not believe a shred of it. I mean know it so well that I could complete the exam: eyes closed, hands tied behind my back, and somehow still ace it!

I'm talking about knowing something so well that I'd regurgitate it to walk through doors, into spaces and wield it to avoid harm. All the while knowing that much of what I had been taught to regurgitate was all bullshit, baloney, worthless ideas, misleading concepts, and someone else's view of the world. Society's complicated belief systems and ideologies that I secretly rejected.

When I was a small child, my mother had us participate in cleaning the house. She is a woman that needs and expects things to be clean and tidy at all times. Needless to say, I hated having to mop the kitchen floors every week. Then somewhere around five or six years old, after huffing and puffing about the chore, my mother made it very clear. That is to say, she made it abundantly clear by announcing to me. "You don't have to like it, you just have to do it."

Those words uttered by my mother caused me to think and Wonder what it meant and how it could be applied. A week later, it dawned on me. Like an aha moment, a realization, or a spiritual enlightenment. In that moment, I had come to know and understand that no one had access to my mind. I had the freedom to think and feel whatsoever I wanted and whatsoever I chose. The realization that not even my mother could make me feel or believe in something freed my mind. My newfound realization lacked the power to free my body of its daily chores, for they had to be done in spite of my personal thoughts surrounding them. Although I hadn't heard the word by then, my adult self will translate that concept into the word comply. Comply, meaning, do it even though you hate it, while also not making too much of a fuss.

Not long after my realization, I was introduced to a woman with a ghoulish religious zeal and outlook. The cult woman told me about her scary god. I believed her for a bit. That is until she said that I was "destined to hell" for my behavior. Hmm…

My earlier enlightenment came in handy for when I was introduced to the fanatically religious woman who became a temporary fixture during my childhood. You see, what the zealously religious woman with the sick god didn't know was that I knew real love. My grandmother's love and presence were so loving and pure, that it made the woman's words regarding her hell sound fishy. Having had a taste of real love and acceptance through my grandmother made the cult lady's demands and punishments sound like a prison and feel like one too.

Though still a child, I was too wise to accept the unhealthy restrictions placed on me by a cult culture. My grandmother doted, adored and loved on me in a way that felt safe, warm and electrically divine that I knew deep down inside of my prepubescent gut, tucked away in my soul that I was a good kid. And good kids who've experienced true love cannot be tricked into believing that they'd ever end up in somcone's hcll to bc eternally punished. "Bullshit", my heart said to me. My lips refrained from making this understanding known to anyone at the time.

The other thing the woman living in her own fiery hell didn't know was that I loved language, so I made up my own. When I was told to say please forgive me from my sins before the cult leader, I changed its meaning. Within the language I created that sentence meant "shut up crazy lady, we all know you're the one in and going to the place you have created for me. Plus, you are not my mother."

It took years, well into my adulthood to realize what child abuse that was. To tell a child they have to change who they are in order to avoid the hell that the loveliest people in his world had never mentioned as a possibility is unbelievably cruel. What kind of person tells a child that?

Lucky for me, I never believed her rubbish while I solidly and secretly held within my gut, the knowing that I was a good kid. So I participated in praising her god in a performance that could have granted me at least five Oscars and 2 Academy Awards. So, when I said "praise god" to the cult lady, it simply meant "fuck off". Then I smiled softly and warmly.

I said you're such a nice woman to be around, but in my language, that meant "I'm glad you're not my mother, otherwise I would have believed and your rubbish."

You see, that is how I complied. I regurgitated the verses, the commentary about hellfire and abominations all while not believing a lick of it. I complied as a means of being left alone and to avoid her ever increasing punishments. I learned to speak that woman's cult language as a means of my own survival.

I somehow had the wisdom at an early age to understand that anyone that cursed me with hell wasn't meant for me to follow nor emulate and that such a person is therefore incapable of determining whether I am a sinner.

"Amen" meant "get lost", then I'd hug her.

This skill to use someone's language and change the meaning so that I could say what I wanted gave me power.

So when I entered the working world doing jobs that I hated among people who often hated themselves or their jobs, I complied yet again. This time in the so-called professional world, I did it with a different sort of grace, posture, and lightheartedness. However, I always found it strangely bizarre how blogs, coworkers and leaders everywhere wrote and talked about imposter syndrome as if it were something that one had to fight or needed to overcome.

Being an impostor was one of my greatest skills as a youngster and as a young professional. I was convinced for a long time that embodying a role that did not belong to me was the only way to make money and thrive in society.

You see, the hellfired woman taught me what none of the books I read could ever reveal to me. She taught me how to kill dragons, tame lions, hypnotize bears and castrate fizards. She taught me not to fear because somewhere along the line, I came to realize that I was in control.

You see, that woman would dish out so many demands and punishments in the name of her god and it's hell. So when she told me to tell my real mother that her lifestyle was going to send her to hell, I'd reply by saying "okay." In my language that meant 'fuck off I'm not going to hurt my mother for your devilish god. The only one going to the land you profess is you.' Then, I'd smile warmly.

I knew early on that the hellfired woman wanted something from me and I wanted nothing from her. Placing all the power in my adolescent hands. Like any adolescent, I had a know-it-all attitude that I cleverly kept hidden from view. I talked back using my self created language. I pretended to be sweet while being annoyed. I pretended to care when I didn't. I pretended to believe her words, but I didn't.

I did all of this to stroke the hellfired women's ego. Pet, pet, pet…

You see, when someone forced me to be someone I was not, it put me behind the wheel. My compliance became the reward for the beast. Like a treat to my dog, it soothed the beast's ego, calmed its nerves and made me safe. I'd give and strategically withdraw my compliance to control her whims and devilish ways. I could tell she felt good and in control by my supposed compliance. It all served to keep the beast off my back as best I could. All beasts like treats.

Pet, pet, pet…

You see, to kill any beast or fizard, you learn its language, pretend to believe the rubbish with the good. Then you appear defenseless. That is when the beast leans in and that is when you pet the beast.

Pet, pet, pet…

As useful as it has been to have developed a chameleon-like skin to be anyone I chose, doing things I hated; I can do it no longer. Although it afforded me the ability to see the world through the lens of others, regardless of how founded or baseless their beliefs. My means of survival as a child fostered a great skill within me. I became a child who could pinpoint and understand a person's belief system fairly quickly and see the discrepancies within it. Furthermore, it gave me the understanding that a person's identity is determined by their belief system.

As youngster, I became highly aware and attuned to the multitude of belief systems that existed in the world around me. My survival instinct caused me to be less concerned with my own identity because knowing who I had to be in order to earn my safety amongst adults was a critical point of my survival. But the identity shifting somehow never bothered me because I also understood that identities were just like fashion anyhow. You learn which outfits and pieces to wear for each occasion and each moment. Like all the outfits I've worn, I knew I was the wearer.

I am me. That has always been clear. As I changed identities to keep me safe and help me thrive, I was always aware of who I was. As I got older, I learned to stitch together and develop my own ever-evolving belief system. Taking from the good bits and pieces that I acquired from my assumed identities. A conglomeration of only the best, most loving, most freeing and simplest of beliefs. I switched and I replaced my old outdated beliefs with more expansive ones as the years progressed. Like replacing parts in a car to keep it running smoothly and happily in changing times and terrains.

But ultimately, my grandmother gave me a type of love that said "I love you for you. I love you for breathing." Grandma taught me that I didn't have to change myself to be loved, so I pretended as a means of protecting myself and to advance myself within different spaces. Especially within the employment world, I assumed that I was hired to "perform a role", to be the imposter, rather than simply being me.

I knew from my mother's first kiss on the day of my birth and from my grandmother's touch that those who truly love me will never demand that I betray myself. That those who love me would never attempt to send me to imaginary places called hell.

Well, that chameleon phase is finally over, though I still retain the lessons and skills gained as I enter into a new life chapter called: No Pretending.

Those of you in my life who always got the me that I am, please know that I love, adore and cherish you. It has been a blessing to have such people in my life that never expected me to be anything but who I am. No pretending required. My love always showed up in full force when naked and disrobed of the pretense.

But now that I have turned a new leaf, I will no longer be anything or anyone other than who I am.

Boldly, I am who I am. Firmly, I am who I am. Securely, I am who I am. Unflinchingly, I am who I am. Decisively, I am who I am. Decidedly, I am who I am. Lovingly, I am who I am.

And so, I say all that just to say… I hope you the divine and supreme understanding of who you are beyond the outfits and beyond the skins. For I will not pretend is how one says "I love me" and it is how one says *I love you.*

When Is It Time for a Revolution?

Powerfully threatful
The emperor hasn't any gold.
Seemingly mighty
The emperor hasn't any gold.
Needing to hold on, needing to control
The emperor hasn't any gold.
Kept only by tradition, crumbled through disregard
The emperor hasn't any gold.
Power and contriteness failing
The emperor hasn't any gold.
Yet, did the gold matter?

Encased

I don't know why, but I was thinking about butterflies today. I mean I was really thinking about how they all come out of that cocoon. Thinking about what goes through its mind as it realizes it's time to emerge. You know that moment just before the cocoon is broken and a twitch before the butterfly attempts to make that great escape?

What goes on in its head? Ever think about that?

Well, I think about that moment far more than I care to admit. Do you not ever Wonder what the butterfly thinks of itself as it gets ready to see the outside world?

I need you to pause and seriously think about this…

Does the butterfly still believe that it's a caterpillar, or does it know it's a butterfly as soon as it awakens within the darkness?

Moreover, do the caterpillars know that they will one day become a butterfly?

Well, I must tell you, it depends on which caterpillar you ask. You see, there are two kinds of caterpillars in this world. One that dislikes the butterflies for their beauty, flying ability, and flamboyance. In other words, this kind of caterpillar doesn't wish for butterflies to be successful, nor does it wish for the butterflies to be free; fluttering around in over abundant joy. That's the unloving caterpillar.

Now, an entomologist would never tell you this, but I will. Unloving caterpillars produce a fragrance that attracts birds that delight in the sour taste of unloving caterpillars. The birds slowly and meticulously devour their bodies bit by bit, unaware that it's the worst kind of death to a caterpillar.

But that's not the worst part. Usually, when an unloving caterpillar gazes up at a butterfly, it doesn't see its own reflection, recognizes no family ties, nor imagines a harmonious relationship existing between them.

Then there is the second kind of caterpillar. This one starts its life loving every butterfly it sees and wishes it a happy and prosperous life whenever they flutter by. As this loving caterpillar matures, it dreams about becoming a butterfly. As it gets older still, the caterpillar dares to fantasize about becoming a butterfly. In the final stages of the caterpillar's maturity, its fantasies turn into beliefs. The belief that it was destined to be a butterfly and therefore has always been a butterfly.

That's why there is only one type of butterfly. Born from loving caterpillars; the ones that know as soon as they emerge that they have been butterflies forever and always... Eternally.

With this newfound knowing, I'm sure it won't surprise you to learn that unloving caterpillars never become butterflies. Sad thing is those poor caterpillars never knew they had a choice. To love or not to love, "that is the question" as [3]Hamlet so beautifully put it.

---

[3] Referring to William Shakespear's play Hamlet written between 1599 and 1601, in Act 3 Scene one Hamlet says "To be or not to be, that is the question"

Now, before I go any further in this lecture, allow me to state my expert qualifications on the interrelatedness of biology, chemistry, ecology, botany, zoology, physics, love, power and spirituality.

You see, I am someone who always knew that I was a butterfly. I am therefore speaking from firsthand experience. Some circles call this "being vulnerable", for I am exposing my insides by telling you who and what I am and from whom I stem. That is why I always knew I could fly. I knew it because the butterfly knows it, because a loving caterpillar knows it and because I love and adore them both.

But you can only understand someone or something if you love all parts of them unreservedly and unflinchingly. Seeing your whole self in someone or something else is the very definition of love. I am you and you are me.

I am grateful that my heritage stems from a special breed of caterpillars; the ones that turn into butterflies.

And so, I say all that just to say… Let's all make the divine choice to appreciate each other with one simple phrase: I see you emerging. And that is how you say *I love you.*

Crossroads of the Present

Going through
I see good and bad times
Looking back
All I remember is the good
Peppered by lessons
Supporting my growth
Supporting my shine

Let's Start Somewhere

Whoever said there was a beginning was a well-intentioned, yet misguided soul. Within the ancient civilizations upon the landmass we now call Africa, it was common knowledge that you should not trust any bipedal creature that speaks of definite beginnings. For beginnings are arbitrary points in time and space. Beginnings can be moved around, pushed back and forth, moved over and under whenever and however one desires. The selection of the beginning of anything reveals more about the individual than it does the coordinated sequence of events that led up to whatever moment the speaker of definite beginnings speaks of.

Don't believe me? Ask yourself, when does a man's hair begin to recede? Can you give it a specific date and time? Does it begin once those around him start to recognize the hair's departure from the crown? Or does it start once a certain level of maturity or awareness creeps into the skull? Or, does it start with a series of hormonal events that began while he was still in the womb? Does a receding hairline begin with two chromosomes meeting for the first time who then pre-determine which few hairs will fall away first, well before his so-called date of birth? Or does it happen around the time the egg and the sperm are still getting to know each other? And can we go back even further?

Did we all start to speak when we uttered our first words? Or did it begin the moment we started to babble? Or perhaps we all started to speak as we practiced moving our tongue and lips while lounging upside down in amniotic fluid. Or better yet, perhaps we started to speak the day our ancestors yearned for another form of communication. So they encoded our DNA with the necessary components to ensure we could all have the ability to laugh and then tell someone why we're laughing. To smile and then tell someone why we're smiling. To love and then to tell someone why we're loving.

If you have not yet realized it by now, beginnings are endless and true beginnings are bangless.

Did today truly start this morning, or did it begin when I began planning it last week? Are those moments truly separate? Even the greatest goddesses that have ever been imagined still marvel at the absence of the beginning and the blatant hostile absence of endings. That thing that describes all things, everything, including the nothings; still laughs when another bipedal creature with the gift of language somehow has not recognized that beginnings and endings are mathematically and physically impossible to separate and encapsulate.

Perhaps, the most important step in the advancements of the Hooraata was ability to finally conceptualize the simultaneous presence and absence of beginnings and endings. A phenomenon best described as a bending.

What new universalistic advancements may be on the horizon when modern day descendants of the Hooraata, as a broad collective, realize that our brains are the only ones capable of this feat?

Furthermore, we see prehistoric leaning school districts and political ideologies that try so incessantly and repulsively to draw a pristine line around that which they call "history" and that which they call "irrelevant to it". However, these two data points are just as arbitrary as beginnings and endings and often attached to a motive. Hence, book bans that have existed throughout the history of book making.

Think about it, when did the history of land start for the land on which I was born? I assume some may say it started with conquest, others may say it began with a revolutionary war. While others may point to stories told by indigenous populations long before the arrival of any Mayflower. But of course, there may be a geographer or two, who may point us to a supercontinent oft called Pangea as the start. Thus, completely ignoring common political and social agreements on where to place the beginning of the landmass once called the "New World".

To what degree will our national dummy quotient worsen as it continues to shrink the box of that which these systems like to call "history"? Such a history can henceforth be referred to as a slithory (pronounced: slithery). The term is meant to churn your gut, as a reminder to think and question beyond the page, image, and words. No offense to the sheep in the room. After all, we all have free choice. To be a sheep or not, was perhaps what [4]Hamlet urged us to question.

However, let's not forget to mention that the stories behind the aforementioned New World, the northern hemisphere, or the seas can never be told in its entirety, nor can it even hint at the partial story of anything that ever was or will be. If the histories told fail to mention the Pink Lady, born Louis Driscoll - a woman who stood as one of the greatest representations of what it means to love all things and therefore to know all things. May we all gaze upon her

---

[4] Referring to William Shakespear's play Hamlet written between 1599 and 1601, in Act 3 Scene one Hamlet says "To be or not to be, that is the question"

constellation that is arranged in a three-dimensional placement of galaxies. However, to help our physical eyes experience her, she ensured that the color pink could be seen throughout the earth and beyond.

And I say all that just to say... Praise to the Pink Lady. And that's how you say *I love you.*

Death

I don't mean for this to be silly, not even a profound philosophical question, nor a futile debate about pedantry. But why do some things not hurt when they're supposed to? In other words, why do we sometimes expect pain and not get it and why do we not feel pain at the moment we expect it?

Who has taken a fall or a tumble, only to laugh with a friend, dust yourself off and continue along their merry way? Continuing with an exchange of stories and banter, that is, until your dear friend yells out "Dear Wonder! You're bleeding!"

In full disbelief, you smile and look down with a peculiar Wonder. Thinking "how on earth did I not feel my ripped flesh, nor sense the bleeding blunder? How on earth did this abrasion escape my senses?"

You Wonder. It Wonders. I Wonder.

Then upon observation of the red drip, your brain is triggered into finally feeling pain, when there was no pain to be felt before the sighting. Strange, isn't it? The moment you recognize that you're not recognizing, is the moment you recognize. Translation: the pain waits patiently upon your eyes to fool you. Fool you into thinking that you are, or somehow were, supposed to feel pain. Such pain is best referred to as illusory pain. That is to say, the pain arrived because the eyes encouraged it to show up, not because the pain was, in fact, there.

As introverted as pain is inclined to be, it will seep in every time you call it. The act of wondering why you don't feel any pain, summons the ache. Slowly but surely, you start to feel the pain you summoned.

How might the events have been any different if you had looked down and your knee jerk reaction never expected any pain? What I am explicitly asking is: what if you could be reprogrammed into having different knee jerk thoughts? Would you do it?

At that point, does the pain go away, or does it never arrive? Two sides of the same coin. A not-so beginning and a not-so ending.

You Wonder. It Wonders. I Wonder.

Perhaps your friend never should have pointed it out.

On the other hand, you've never seen a ritual until you've seen the mental and physical acrobatics that some of us engage in as the phlebotomist prepares the needle, to help our bodies endure the impending sting. Having high expectations for pain, the needle penetrates the skin. Oftentimes the sting is either underwhelming or the stinging pain completely absent.

Where's the pain? You Wonder. It Wonders. I Wonder.

Could it have been the phlebotomist's skill of hand or could it have been the ritual? The way you psyched yourself out, or the way you gripped the chair while conjuring up better days in your head. How might this knowing change the way we worry - change the way we fret?

…Don't you just Wonder?

Then we have the supposed pain of impending death. Ever Wonder if the knee-jerk reaction for many of us to fear death, is a knee-jerk programmed response? To be more specific - and not to beat around the bush - but does our culture, to any degree, teach us to fear death because we are not naturally nor organically inclined to do so?

Along this vein of thought, the fear of death taking residence within our minds seems out of place, unless faced by a [5]"true lion, tiger, or a bear", of course. Digging deeper, does the fang toothed beast truly trigger a fear of death within us, or does it trigger an intense appetite for life? Some can argue that it's a bit of both. However, if you survive the beasts, the fear eventually fades; as I am sure Dorthy would agree

What happens when a people, a culture, and a society stop teaching and preaching the fear of death and then what happens to a nation's death row? What happens for you, the individual, when you stop fearing death. You Wonder. It Wonders. I Wonder.

And I say all that just to say… Reprogramming the mind is an individual pursuit and you surely possess that ability. And that is how you say *I love you.*

---

[5] "Lions, tigers and bears" is a reference to the line made famous by the character Dorthy, played by Judy Garland, in Wizard of Oz. A film released in 1939

Hear My Cry

I Wonder
I Wonder
I Wonder as Wonder's Wonder
What Wonder am I?
Wonder me
To Wonder Wonder
Wonder that

Creating a Kinder World Garden

A great essay written by Rober Fulghum once said "all I need to know, I learned in kindergarten" (1986) and I'd have to agree, or at least admit that I can find no sensical argument against it. Kindergarten… Oh, that suspicious letter "t" in kindergarten reflecting its linguistic origin. Having roughly the same pronunciation in German, the language from which it came. Direct translation being quite exactly as it might sound to the English hearing ear, in spite of its German spelling.

The direct German translation is "children's garden", but is a children's garden really any different than a kinder garden? A… Kinder... Garden.

With English being my second language after mastering the artful language of cooing and kahing, German just made sense as the next tongue to acquire. I swear it was an easy language to learn because of its practicality. In short, it made so much sense to my uniquely formed neural connections.

In my mind, children and kinder [English] had always been the same thing. A type of synonym. So, in spite of its slightly different pronunciation as the word jumps from English to German, when I learned that Kinder [German] meant children in German, it was an easy association to make.

Where in the world are children not kinder than the rest of the population? Why should the word kind ever exist as an unrelated word to child? After all, if you could point at nature's most pure alchemized example of kindness, wouldn't most of us point to small children in a grassy field or garden?

I am absolutely convinced that the most magical place on earth is not a place with talking mice; it's a kindergarten playground. The kindest garden of them all. A place where freedom and wonder are still [6]ringing. Where there is no one there looking to financially profit off of your existence, nor efforts. Where the prominent currencies are play and laughter. A place where relationships possessing an extra helping of love and giggles can easily qualify you as best friends.

But there - amidst snotty noses and squeals - all that we need in order to be what our species requires for the next phase of our evolution, is to be observed within a garden of children. That is, in case we so happened to have forgotten the lessons of our youth.

The most important lessons being: share and share alike. As Fulghum so beautifully pointed out.

Thinking back, I recall my older brother making it to the kinder garden a year before I did. Thus convincing my 4-year old mind to believe that he was the smartest kid ever, because he got to go away to learn all day. Surprisingly, when I made it to the kindest of gardens, the lessons reflected what my brother shared with me as we played together at home. We shared a room, the toys, the socks, books, clothing and the list goes on.

---

[6] Referencing the words of the Honorable Dr. Martin Luther King's 'I Have a Dream' speech from Aug 28,1963 at the Lincoln Memorial wherein he repeatedly declares "Let freedom ring…"

In short, everything was shared, from the physical objects that surrounded us to the nonphysical world that composed our thoughts and imaginations. A special realm, a world where everything belonged to everyone was the bedroom of my childhood. It's funny, as I reflect upon those tender years, I recall that I had no concept of ownership within that microcosm that I once called a bedroom.

Not too dissimilar, all the children shared the monkey bars, puzzles and building blocks when I attended the kinder garden.

Sharing wasn't simply a rule in my toy-strewn bedroom nor the school yard, it was our childhood custom. Thinking back… What delightful, pleasing, or lovely things in my childish world could not be shared?

Sharing and caring was the name of the game:
- Share your thoughts, but do it nicely and kindly
- Share the ball
- Only take a few so that there's enough for everybody
- Share the win
- Share what you know
- Help someone up when they fall, then ask if they'd like a hug

We shared just about everything there was, including our warm arms. So, it's bewildering how the notion of owning slowly seeped into my growing mind. The world and educational system seemed to collude to remind me of what was mine and what was not, thus making sharing a custom of ever decreasing value within the social order of older teens and seemed to decrease even further into adulthood. How did my generation allow this to continue unchecked? And why was the generation before us so married to this idea of sole ownership of anything?

As the summers came and went, and as Crayons were replaced with pens, I began to ask myself: What happened to sharing? What happened to sharing the world that we clearly all share? What is it about our history, that we would develop a world where more is done to legalize the proliferation or notion of owning, rather than the rampant expansion of shared resources and comforts?

And I say all that just to say… There is a bold loving curious child inside of you and it's time to let it lead. And that is how you say *I love you.*

Putting That on Everything

No tear uncried, no moan unuttered, nor word left bottled
No joy unsquealed, no laugh held in, nor smile withheld

That's the life I intend to live

Lacing up my shoes with the arrival of each new adventure
Emptying my seat at the next song, outstretched hands and aimless
hips leading the way

That's the life I intend to live

Hummingbirds shall always have my full attention
Flowers, my utmost grace
Mighty trees, my deepest Aww

That's the life I intend to live
I do solemnly swear.

Message in a Bottle

<u>Qualifications:</u>
While handsome goes without saying - a man loving enough to pour me cups of tea brewed in the knowledge of the most elusive stars until he has nothing left to pour, but plenty more pats on the back to give - must be explicitly stated!

Now, let's not be hasty to discuss compensation, for one of the few things I can offer is to be your sponge. I'll listen, I'll soak it all up and my plate shall not reveal any evidence of the sweetness you served and I shall say thank you every time.

Without you, it can sometimes feel that "being a man" is akin to recreating the wheel, rather than upgrading the notion. I know someone has done this before! So why am I roaming the wilderness of this planet without any knowledge of how any wise man with love in his heart has done it before me?

I don't want no stinking heaven; I'm not even asking for money this time. I'm saving my next big wish on a father, fathers, or any man anywhere to invest the best parts of who he is, that I may be a better who-I-am with a clearer understanding of how I can make a dream or fantasy enter my reality.

Guide me to know all you really know. Thus, granting me insights to grow wings, take flight, dance playfully in the most tremendous of waves, laugh at daggers pointed my way, and giggle every time I see the worse-est storm drawing near.

Of course, none of this would be complete without your sack of survival secrets; containing morsels of candy-wrapped wisdom. How to ignite and put out fires of any variety, how to dive deeper, and to be a safe place to all things. Make this seed I carry burst, sprout, and bloom the most beautiful unbloomable bloom and we shall call it your creation.

Needless to say, a role of such esteemly prominence shan't go unpaid. For I have an endless treasure trove of kisses, accounts are dripping with a kind of adoration this world has never seen, and every time you look at me - I do solemnly swear - you'll see Wonder whenever my eyes meet yours.

All of this wealth that I've amassed is ready to be spent, with not a sentiment left. It's all yours Mister Poppins, if only you make yourself known.

Sincerely,

Your patiently waiting son

Love Defined

Love is
knowing I am safe
knowing I am free
knowing I can be kind
and that Love is me

Bravery

You know, I was sitting down thinking about all the risks we'd take as kids. I remember enduring that common parental speech in the parking lot, then having the nerve to ask for something as soon as we walked into the store. We'd slam car doors for "no goddamn reason". But seriously, we took all kinds of risks as kids. We'd take: "letting the hot air into the house for the 15th time today" kind-of-risk. Opening the fridge when "there ain't nothing there for you!" kind-of-risk." Staying out after the streetlights came on kind-of-risk. And the worst offense of them all… Won't take my ass back to bed kind-of-risk... Y'all can't hear me in the back!! Our childhood was full of risks, it was exciting.

So now I'm sitting here wondering: when did taking a risk become so scary that it'd stop us in our tracks? So it got me thinking about one simple word. Bravery. And I believe that everything we have ever learned about bravery in our movies and fairytales have been all wrong. True bravery is not simply a word, it's a moment and an act of freedom.

I remember being forced to eat greens as a kid- and although my mouth wouldn't dare say it, my body and frown said with raging seriousness: "fuck you, I ain't gonna eat it. Ain't no way in hell." "AIN'T NO WAY IN HELL!" If you've ever said it or felt it, THAT IS BRAVERY. Did you ever go to a party as a teenager or been somewhere you weren't supposed to be as a youngster? Then look at the time or saw the darkness of night outside and realized. Shit! It's time to go before I'm in trouble! But you didn't. Mmm hmm, you stayed. All while feeling the terror of the pending consequences and not giving a shit, all at the same time. That's when the party truly comes to life, because that is when you decide this crime is gonna be worth it, allowing you to enjoy the space like never before. I choose me. THAT IS BRAVERY.

I actually remember the first time I felt that spark of bravery. I was a small child, peeking out from beneath the covers, too frightened to even look at the dark, not realizing that the darkness that comforted me under my sheets was the same one outside. The dark was a scary place as a kid. But I can still remember that feeling inside of my gut that gave me the thrust I needed to hop outta that bed, then race through the darkness to find comfort in my mother… So I've realized today, that bravery is simply the feeling you possess while taking a leap, while you're simultaneously sitting in fear, all while knowing the potential consequences and not giving a shit. It was inside of us from the beginning. Think about it, no seriously, think about it. If baby you could do it, then baby, THIS YOU can do it too.

And so, I'm saying all that just to say… I wish you the bravery of a child as you race through the dark. And that is how you say *I love you.*

Love Ain't

Love doesn't harm
Nor come with strings attached
Love doesn't resurrect the Big Bad Wolf
Nor the smile of the Wicked Witch of the West
Love doesn't cease to be symbiotic
Nor leave you uncertain
Love doesn't growl when it already sees you're scared
Nor frown at your thriving
Love just ain't

For Better or Worse

Why are some things far better than what we're told, while other experiences far worse than anyone cares to admit? Looking back. Taking inventory. Thereby, uncovering the countless ways I've been told something would be terrible, yet turned out to be a splendidly remarkable moment in time. How or why did I ever believe the naysayers? What about the half a million times I mindlessly believed that something would be grand and it wasn't? How or why did I ever believe the yaysayers?

I spent a good portion of my life taking morsels of fizdom rather than wisdom from the so-called "well-intentioned", yet ill informed, yay- and naysayers. Two categories, two boxes that I had no business taking from. One can call it a simple case of believing in someone's outdated beliefs, or perhaps we can call it: Taking what doesn't belong to you.

The two categories seemed to plague my decisions and therefore curbed my desires, taking me down the path that wasn't meant for me. However, I thank Wonder for the automatic course corrector that has been in my life. Built into the chemistry of my body, the insights of this mind, and the sight of this heart, Wonder is there providing revelation and direction meant for the proper unfolding of my unearthed desires.

To whom do our desires belong anyhow? To whom do my desires belong? I ask

Somehow Wonder is pervasively present, adjusting my direction with the precision of a fine-tuned compass, as a not-so-subtle means of reminding me to choose me and my longings. That is to say, dive, walk, crawl or at least tiptoe along the path of my brightening desires.

Desires. Do they truly grow brighter or do they simply get closer with our steps? Serving as a guiding light.

And I say all that just to say… Allow true Wonder from within to guide you to your highest fulfillment. And that is how you say *I love you*.

A More Appropriate Name

We've all fallen or slipped, for Mother Gravity's mind never lapses nor does she forget her nature. It's funny how we've been speaking and smiling on this earth for so long, but has anyone, be it creatively, religiously, or scientifically been able to define, depict or display a godthing that is grander than gravity? Gravity is a phenomenon, a thing, that we all simultaneously feel and interact with. We cannot see it, nor can we deny its might.

Who or what has never interacted with gravity?

Is there no story of a godthing out there that can make the phenomenon of gravity seem unremarkable or not so novel? Is there nothing else or something else that we can all simultaneously feel or experience? What if there is a thing or a collection of things that will never be felt nor realized until someone finally points it out? What if we could all feel or experience that "something else" if we all stopped taking our senses for granted? Similar to a fish finally recognizing that it's in water, what if we could finally point out that thing? And could it change the species, allowing us to evolve into the intelligent beings we seek in the sky?

Time has always told us that the poets are often ahead of their time, but I like to take that to mean: poets exist not just at the edge of thought, but they create it. Thus, helping scientists divert their attention to more important pursuits and help the living create grander and more loving gods and goddesses. Thereby, paving the way to aid the masses in leading more meaningful lives.

I therefore offer that one thing that is holding gravity in place and connects the species. It can only be described as Beautiful Imaginings, or more specifically, Wonder. Wonder is the one thing connecting all of us to all of it. Like love and joyous laughter, Wonder cannot yet be measured by our present technology, but I can sense when it's present and it moves me every time. Like loving warmth, it cannot be quantified by any standardized scale, nor can it be faked if you're paying attention. But this apparatus that I carry, this body and heart, knows when it's there.

The measure of a society, is the measure by which all of its inhabitants are encouraged to and equipped with every resource the person needs to continue in the feeling and exploration of Wonder. The kind of Wonder that we were born with. Like a fierce race to the moon and with the haste produced by the threat of tardiness, every government, every school, every scholar and everyone still breathing should inquire this most necessary series of questioning: How does a society chip away at an individual's personal pursuit to Wonder? How might a society narrow one's range of wonderment and how do we curtail it? What changes when educational systems become more concerned with encouraging natural Wonder and begin to disregard useless and unnatural conformity?

How much of our health and well-being individually and worldly can be impacted, predicted and predetermined by the degree to which we are able to pursue our Beautiful Imaginings, our Wonder?

Could Wonder, that is to say, could our measure or degree of Beautiful Imaginings be used as a proxy for such things as anxiety, depression, contentment, peace, joy, or happiness? Can we, like children, maintain our zest for life simply by not turning away from our Beautiful Imaginings? This is the kind of Wonder that causes the little ones among us to ask "what is that?" and "what is that?", followed by "but why?" and "how come?". All while hoping and expecting splendid or even magical responses.

But being so young, the smallest children are still learning to articulate what they are truly feeling inside when they first start to point with their little fingers in an attempt to investigate their surroundings. For when a child asks "what is that?", it means "what is that thing I feel when I see that?"

From that viewpoint, all things can be summed up in just a few categories: love, flight, growth, change, roots, branches, waves and cheer. Or simply call it Wonder.

Call it Wonder.

And so, I say all that just to say… Let's activate the Wonder inside us by pointing out the wonderfulness in someone else. And that is how you say *I love you.*

Presence

Looking there and looking here
Looking there and looking here
Looking back and looking forth
Looking up and looking down
You are everything in between

Love in Fantasies

Many people have texted and messaged me about my little nephew Troy, with both laughs and tears. And the story seemed to resonate with so many people. Thank you for seeing yourself in that story, because your sharing allows me to see myself in yours. That is the clever moment we see each other and realize that I am you and you are me and therefore, we are one. THAT IS CALLED LOVE. So when I think of little Troy back at the pool playing daredevil; yet again. I will consider it my biggest joy, my greatest pleasure, and my unending duty to hold from him the secret that he cannot swim.

Do you love yourself like that? To hold that kind of secret from yourself? It makes limitations appear as mere illusions when you think of it like that. And so, my hands will always be there to pull him up whenever he needs air, all while keeping the precious secret. For if he were to ever be shaken into learning that he cannot swim, let's face it. That becomes the day we all have to be a lot more careful around the pool, isn't it? Because that is the moment his whole life and the whole world around him begins to change with that knowing. The pool will never be the same again. Yet the terrible and most magical part about it is that once he learns that he cannot swim, I begin to believe it for myself. The more I get to watch Troy live his life without seeing his limitations, allows me to live without seeing mine. His fantasy becomes mine and mine his. Intertwined and Interdependent.

When I think of our ancestors, the ones that made it over to this place called the 'land of the free', but to us, it had to be the land of our fantasies. So in my dreams, and in my fantasies and the stories whispered long long ago, our ancestors told stories about the ones who dove into the sea, grew fins, and swam away. Only later to tell stories about those who flew away to freedom. Then somewhere along the line, the wisest elders of them all - with the wisdom of a thousand lives - realized it was time to keep a secret. Therefore, the trans elders of our communities spoke. And they said 'don't tell the children they are slaves… let them believe in their fantasies that they may not see their limitations.' When you look at it in that way, you begin to realize that you are the fantasy of your ancestors and they are yours. Two fantasies intertwined in time and space…. Interdependent.

I believe that we as Black folk have the luxury of obtaining the things that we want, not because we believe in what we see, but because we get to believe in the the fanta-SEE. You SEE? This is why our ancestors have worked so hard in the background to keep their names out of the nation's silly textbooks, because our ancestors were always meant to live in our fanta-SEES and we in theirs. That is our heritage.

And so, I'm saying all that just to say… I wish you the extraordinary opportunity to believe in your fantasies, that you may not see the illusions of your limitations… And that is how you say *I love you.*

Glimpses

I'm so glad that I was introduced to cross country running as a small unsure teen. I wasn't sure that I could do it, but I wanted to do something that made me cool and popular. However, no one told me that I chose the wrong sport for those ends. But it didn't matter in the long run because cross country loved me and I returned the sentiment. I never actually came in at first place and that didn't matter either. I loved running. It felt like an opportunity to fly and stretch myself.

Cross country was a place that created space for me to experience myself in brand new ways. Deep inside of me, my heart asked "What am I capable of?" and Miss Cross Country replied "here's the path, see it for yourself". Had it not been for what I had seen and experienced along those winding and looping courses, I don't believe I would have followed my gutly intuition at some of the most critical moments of my life. Each long, sweltering, grueling, panting run, getting progressively longer with each passing year felt like a leap of faith. Who knew Miss Cross Country had anything to do with faith? And who knew cross country had anything to do with jumping?

One of the things that I remember from those years, is that many of those 3-mile races that zigzagged and looped around in a variety of ways. Some more creatively than others. These meandering races would often start and finish at the same line, taking us down into valleys where we'd lose sight of where we had come from. Which is to say, we had lost sight of where we were going. But after figureeighting and circling around the course a few times, we'd get to see glimpses of the finish line in the distance. My mother, dragging my siblings in tow, would cheer me on at so many of those races. Appearing at one stretch of the race and then shortcutting to appear at the next. And what seemed to be a practical joke or tease, the most creative courses would have us loop past the finish line a time or two. The target would be so close and then be so far away, yet again.

Just like the targets of my dreams and the dreams of my fantasies, and glimpse of my mother along the route. My visions come in and out of view as I navigate the path of life. Providing me glimpses of what is and what will be. Just keep running is the motto. That is to say, enjoy the view as you embark along the journey. All it takes is one foot at a time and the lovely things you saw along the way will be there at the finish line.

And so, I say all that just to say... As they come in and out of view, let every vision and every passing fantasy be a reminder that you are that much closer to reaching your prize. And that is how you say *I love you.*

I Am a Snowman

When I was in the fourth grade, I pretended to be a snowman. So much in fact that I somehow believed that I had become one. Even wrote a poem about it for Mrs. Brooks class back in 1991, part of which read:

I am white and live on snow
I Wonder if I could walk
I hear leaves falling
I see reindeer running
I want a hat so kids can play around me
I am white and live on snow

I pretend to melt a lot
I feel cold living on snow
I touch a lot of snowflakes
I worry about how I won't melt
I cry when the sun comes up
I am white and live on snow

Words from the little ol' me exactly 30 years ago.

You know, as a snowman, you often feel stuck, frozen in place wanting to move, but can't. Wanting to laugh, but can't. Wanting to cry, but can't.

But after a while, none of that matters anymore, for the joy and laughter you bring to the world is enough to make up for all of the things you supposedly cannot do.

Ever seen a sad abused child smile? Britton, the snowman has. Ever seen an old, strict, grouchy old person soften when no one else was looking? Britton, the snowman has. Ever seen an estranged or tormented couple find a moment of joy and playfulness when they thought all love between them had been lost? Britton, the snowman has.

You see, when this is your life and how you get to interact with the world, it's hard to imagine yourself as anyone or anything else. So you hold onto your identity as the snowman for dear life! Fighting the rays of the sun, resisting the winds, and trying to stand tall in the midst of a snow fight. For snowballs directed at a snowman don't feel like inclement weather, they feel like an unprovoked and unfair war.

The long-held secret about snowmen is that they not only see laughter, play and delight nestled alongside and within sorrow, depression and misery, they create it!

Because they are so cold, most do not recognize that a snowman's superpower is warmth. The kind of warmth that is never withheld nor withdrawn, no matter the encounter… Can you do that?

As a snowman, I reveled on the occasions when I'd see my reflection in the window, or in the sunglasses of a passerby. All proud reminders that I am a snowman.

The stationary existence of a snowman caused me to yearn for freedom of movement, so I dreamt of being passing clouds. I yearned for strength, so I dreamt of being a mighty wave and fantasized about bursting through dams. When snowstorms descended upon my exposed form, I fantasized about being a calm soothing stream. And during the moments I took cheerfulness for granted, I dreamt of being an uncontrollable stream of tears and on other occasions, I dreamt of quenching thirst.

So here I am at nearly 40 years old being revisited by the snowman of my youth and I am pleased to hear that he has matured into a heightened awareness of beingness.

Now, in passing moments of clarity, he realizes that he is not just a snowman. In fact, he is every snowman, snowwoman, snowchild, snow trench, snowball, snow castle and snowthing on the block. Simultaneously.

In deeper moments of clarity, the snowman recognizes that he or she has no real gender to speak of. For in his newfound maturity, the snowman sees snow fall, then realizes that it is made from a collection of unique beautiful snowflakes; with their own stories of how they were formed in the sky above.

So once the snowman understood itself to be the snow in every direction, it only took a brief moment for the snowman to recognize and come into its essence.

The day the snowman came into knowing that it is and always was water, is the day it came into its true nature and was reminded of its history. For water consciously decided to become snow, so that it could one day have the experience of a snowman. And in so doing, have the grand opportunity to see and experience the world from a different vantage point. Even water is playfully curious about how the universe works and how it can participate in expanding love within it.

You see, the snowman is forever changed on the day it realizes that every dream and every fantasy it ever had, were just as much memories of its past as they were visions of its future.

The snowman serves as a reminder not to let the mirror, nor our titles distract us from our true essence. Our nature.

And so, I say all that just to say… You are far more than what can be seen by the naked eye and I hope you know that too. And that is how you say *I love you*.

Choices

Some do not know they are human, so they
Create weapons
Some do not know they are human, so they
Find reason to shoot
Some do not know they are human, so they
Find reason to hate
Some do not know they are human, so they
Fight
Some do not know they are human, so they
Find good reason for authorities to kill
Some do not know they are human, so they
War
Some do not know they are human, so they
Find their morality in the laws of their times
Some do not know they are human.

However unpopular, I choose to be human
And therefore, an expression of love

Pleasure

How or why did I ever pause to deny you your full place in my world? Why did I ever allow myself to turn away from your mischievous smile and your warm embrace? You are everywhere welcome, but oftentimes denied entry.

The modern world uses technological phrases such as, "access denied." But how could any of us be so foolish? You are an element far more pervasive than air, more common than comets, more expansive than the furthest reaches of the galaxy. Far more spacious than outer space.

How brilliant and bright you are.

Somehow possessing the ability to be everywhere but also trapped in nowhere. Leaving behind traces of your immeasurable existence, experienced in passing moments, in moments yet seen and hidden within moments past. A manifestation that exists as a trace, hardly a residue, but evident and profound in each and every way.

You touch my heart and tickle my toes, yet you have no hands. You hold me close, yet you haven't any arms to speak of. You kiss me tenderly, yet absent are your lips.

Like water, you rain down over me, flow through my veins, splash me unexpectedly with laughter and you flow like a determined eternal stream. All while containing the power to burst through dams. Like water, you are quenching, yet wet you are not. Though contained in a moment, you are unbottleable. Elusive yet ever present. But only if we let you in.

We often fool ourselves into thinking that letting you in is so complicated. But an entity, as timeless and as multidimensionally pervasive as thee, cannot be pushed aside nor rejected forever.

All we can do in these mortal bodies is disregard your presence and on other occasions we may allow ourselves to believe we cannot dance with you and delude ourselves into believing that we cannot have you. A type of willful ignorance, or perhaps faulty programming adopted from cultural surroundings.

We hear you tapping at the front door, yet have been known to appear indifferent to the knock. Pretending not to hear a thing.

Yet you are patient and kind and don't take our ignorance personally. Your friendship is always waiting in the shadows, as well as the light. Constantly springing forth and drawing in.

True pleasure. The kind that reaches into and out of our hearts is ours to claim only if we dare to revel in you. Guiltless, we learn to adore you.

And so, I say all that just to say… It is not a matter of letting pleasure in. Pleasure, my friend, is a matter of acknowledging its presence and realizing deep within you that you are always and forevermore deserving of it. And that is how you say *I love you.*

The Future is Here

One small thing I've learned as a writer is that it's nearly impossible to write a book from beginning to end, but to my comfort and great pleasure, that'd be the most boring way to write a book anyhow. In fact, boring as hell! I'm writing a book and chapters 1-3 are done, I skipped chapters 4 and 5, to start chapter 6 and the final chapter is in my head still waiting to be written. Leaving gaps throughout the unfinished book. So, the challenge becomes coming up with a clever way to stitch together the chapters with a seamless storyline.

It can take some writers weeks, days, or months to overcome this peculiar thing called writer's block. Writer's block has come to mean that you have no more ideas. It's frustrating and sometimes enraging not to have any material. But I know, it actually means that you are waiting for an answer. So, I've learned that all you have to do is think for less than a minute about those chapters filling in and being stitched together. Think about how you want those chapters to flow and how the emotional content of the storyline will surge, swell and contract as missing chapters unfold.

Then simply leave it alone. Go on about my business. Walk the dog… go get the mail… take the food out the freezer. Shit, eat that snack. Yeah, I said it. Eat... That... Snack. Relax your mind regarding the topic, drop it for a while… Then one day, all of a sudden. You'll be doing the most mundane thing, like driving home from work, taking out the trash, thinking about what to make for dinner and then whoosh. The idea comes to mind of how to stitch the pieces together.

Now, if we writers can do this with our books. How much more can we all do this with our lives? Stitching together the things that have already happened to the things we wish to happen. The answers are always inside you.

And so, I say all that just to say… I hope in both your roughest and happiest hours, when you need that answer, that you give the situation the respect it deserves by simply calling it: a temporary writer's block… And that is how you say *I love you.*

Footsteps

Going through
I see good and bad times
But mostly darkness
Haze
Unable to see beyond my next step

Looking back
All I remember is the good
Peppered by the lessons
Seeds
Giving way to growth
Whose fruits I now eat

Inspiration

Being told that I could 'be anything I wanted to be' sounded like a magical phrase. Don't you remember they told us we could be anything we wanted to be and they always made becoming the president seem like the highest and most noble achievement of them all?

Come on now, that's the most inspirational thing they can come up with? Who made up the notion that becoming the president is the highest endeavor we could ever dream of achieving? And I say, why set our sights so low?

You're my inspiration. I've looked up to you from the very first day I met you. That's why I love you. By simply watching you grace this world with your presence is a blessing to all of us that know you. You are the very representation of "you can be anything you want to be". Doesn't get mo' better than that.

The beauty of your nature is undeniable.

Having the opportunity to see you evolve into the person that you've always wanted to be gives me the courage to do the same. The world said you couldn't do it, but look at you. You did it anyway. You are a badass! Unfucking-stoppable nobility you are.

And so, I'm saying all that just to say… Thank you for loving yourself so sincerely that you dared to be you, and in doing so, you freed me... And that is how you say *I love you.*

The Birds and the Bees and the Flowers

We can no longer be blind to the story of the birds and the bees. All these centuries and this world has been blind to what nature has been teaching us. For, it isn't a story of copulation nor seduction, although they both have merit in any society. The story actually begins with a strong mighty tree that bears sturdy branches and twigs that grow with the sole intention of one day becoming a nest that cradles and warms new life.

The twig, having never seen an egg, gets great joy and pleasure out of every sighting of birds because somewhere in its gut, the twig and the tree know that they are parts of the bird's lifecycle. The bird loves the tree for the supportive protection of its leaves and branches. The bird loves the tree's majestic flowers, for the flowers are living creative works of art. And the bird is filled with great gratitude when the tree freely nurtures it with fruit. The bird knows that it is the tree and the tree knows it is the bird.

The bird admires the dance of the bees with the flowers. The bees love the support and rest freely offered by the flower's pad. The bees, with a deep sense of gratitude, freely give pollen from afar to the flower as it receives nourishing pollen and nectar from the flower. Thus, representing a symbiotic exchange of resources.

The flower, being as social as it is, always loves a visitor. For the flower uses the beauty deep within itself to attract and express love, not only to flying things, but also to the world. Within this realm, the flower is a simultaneous representation of seduction and beauty; alluring bees and adoring eyes alike. The flower adores the wise bee for its knowledge of the great beyond.

The flower laughs, cries and cheers at the beautiful stories shared by the bee. The flower happily shares its nectar and pollen while expressing gratitude to the bee for delivering messages and insights from far away families of trees. Providing the flower with the knowledge, faith, and inspiration necessary to create fruit, but especially to create seeds. Tiny seeds instilled with a power and love so great that they have the audacity to believe that they will one day become a mighty tree with roots that hold the Earth together.

The fruit loves the bird for freely scattering its seeds far and wide, delivering a message to the world. A message of love and unity with every living thing. It is no Wonder why the tree freely and joyously shares its fruit with anyone and everyone. And as the young seeds and nesting eggs learn from the loving relationships around them, they find ways to make more love and then spread it that much further... Expansion!

The story of the birds and the bees is a story about everyone existing together. Harmoniously and symbiotically. Nurturing each other, loving each other, giving gifts of knowledge and sustenance to each other.

To bask in the joy of life, we all must dance the dance of reciprocity and symbiosis taught to us by the bird, the bee, and the tree that shares its exquisitely lovely flowers with the world. Thus, reminding us that if competition doesn't exist in nature, then it doesn't exist as a healthy part of humanity.

Collaboration is the opposite of competition and competition fights foolishly to oppose collaboration. Competition is greedy because it never reaches the point of satisfaction. That is to say, competition amongst people erodes societies because it requires that there be a loser or someone eradicated, rather than seek ways for us to all be winners. Competition is therefore unnatural, because it goes against the symbiosis that exists within nature and our hearts.

Furthermore, competition is as artificially man-made as the grape flavoring found in sweets and syrups. As the emotional intent behind competition is annihilation. Nations and peoples with competition at the forefront of their efforts represent an invasive human species.

Competition is unnatural to the stars and the sun. Competition is unnatural to Mars and to Venus. Competition is unnatural to the birds and the bees. Competition is the most artificially nonsensical irrationally illogical thought ever thought. Competition is as unnatural and as abstract as a perfectly straight line drawn from here to Kalamazoo. As we all know, there is no way to avoid the inescapable bend of the Earth.

We somehow live amongst people who move through the world only seeing competition and endeavoring to perpetuate it. Should we call them foolish or should we simply call them a barbaric variety of neanderthal?

And here we are at the final frontier, living amongst those who want a particular kind of competition. I have seen this anecdotally and statistically. We live amongst those who want to have a competition of that which we call right and that which we call wrong. As if it can be decided by a vote or puny gavel. Unnatural!

These individuals believe they are drawing a line. On one side it reads "wrong" and on the other side of that line, it reads "right". These individuals believe they can place any issue on whichever side they please. The perpetrators of competition show their amusement of the sport by the arbitrary labeling of right and wrong while making fairness irrelevant within their nomenclature. Such an unnatural line do they draw, not for competition in and of itself, but for power.

Such an unnatural line. This line serves as a barrier, a wall between those who have the power and those who do not. That barrier has been drawn so many times, that it has become so layered that it has created an artificial line of power between the many and the few.

Here we are at the final inning and the fizards are struggling over their final competition, not realizing they have backed themselves into a corner. These foolish fizards - powerless and visionless as they are - believing they can whimsically pick and choose that which we label right and that which we label wrong.

These foolish fizards don't even have the power to grant power, nor extend its reaches. The barrier to power these fizards believe they built is an illusion in their minds and their minds alone. For we all know that nature itself has the power to crush, dismantle, disarm, and degrade any man-made structure with her slightest huff or puff. Be that structure physical or conceptual... Nature's Power!

Then we come to a highly overlooked word that we toss around so often that we forget its true underlying meaning. The word maintenance has one primary assumption and one meaning only. That is... Mother Nature Always Wins. That is why humans struggle against her to maintain that which he thinks he owns. Humans often struggle against her weathering and creative nature.

Mother Nature knows that it is not about right or wrong. Foolish fake phony wizards. Fizards, more like it. It is solely about love, or the lack thereof. To love or not to love, "That is the question" as Hamlet so beautifully put it.

Foolish wizards, that is to say: fizards. These fizards are already on their backs flailing like cockroaches not realizing the game is already over.

Mother nature always wins. That is to say, we live in a world of physical laws.

Mother nature always wins, that is to say, Love wins. That is to say, competition leads directly to extinction as competitors don't know when to stop!! Competitive species will eventually over consume the very resources it needs to survive. Therefore, bringing its own kind into a self-induced extinction.

Want to know what happened to the Neanderthal? Was it competition?

Why did Rome fall? Competition perhaps?

What defines a species of fizards? Competition! Competition of its own making. Foolish.

Fizards are so deeply concerned about not being wrong that they have forgotten what it means to be truly and lovingly right. 'Cause they never cared about being right to begin with, as their fear of being wrong, distorts their gaze. Fearful narcissistic fizards indeed.

That's enough about the few. Now let's talk about the many. The many who don't play silly competitive games. I'm talking about those of us who know better than that. Who turn our noses up at the so-called competition of what is right and what is wrong.

For we have access to the real power of the Universe. The power of symbiosis, meaning collaboration, same as harmony and equivalent to Love. You cannot vote on good nor evil, nor can you defy the laws of gravity, nor stop the continued expansion of the Universe. Like its sister, infinity, love is a limitless power that holds all things together while paradoxically allowing it all to expand and grow at the same time.

The wise know that all true and everlasting things are determined by the force of Love, not power. As we've heard so many a times, God is Love, but don't forget that Love is also God. Love is everlasting and therefore indestructible and piercing. For it shares its power with all who dare to Love and embody Love in all its forms. Existing in a state of constant loving expression.

Love is power, the only one. And to that we say Love: everlasting, indivisible with liberty for all.

Amen

Infinity

Many of us go by so many names, titles and nicknames, that it rarely dawns on us how often we are made to identify with our government issued number. Referred to as a social security number where I'm from. It feels somewhat like a modern-day branding. Instead of burning the skin, you impress the mind. We are compelled to reference that number throughout our entire lives.

It's funny how most of us go by our first name, but our social security number likes to go by its last name. How many of us can recite those last 4 digits faster than spelling our own surname?

We somehow get tricked into believing this assigned arbitrary number stands as a proxy to either our identity, personhood, or ourselves. After all, can those prescribed numbers ever stand as a reference to our very being?

What I find to be peculiar is how easily we can be trained to identify with a randomly assigned number and not recognize the absurdity of that. Now, I recognize everyone's right to hold onto whichever absurdities they wish.

But why not identify with an everlasting infinite number instead? Boundless, limitless, everlasting, multidimensional, endlessly abundant. That infinity. Yes, that one! However, when posed as a question, it serves as a great reminder:

And I say all that just to say... You are as limitless as infinity, so why not identify with it? And that is how you say 'I love you' .

Handkerchiefs, Rag Dolls, and Baby Blankets

Our society doesn't talk enough about the true meaning or the essence of the word "hope", although the word is often flung around like the way we handle handkerchiefs, rag dolls, and baby blankets. Hope is as vital as minerals and as important as the beating of our hearts. And I believe we all know what happens to the so-called "human" that has lost its ability to hope…

To hope is to desire and expect beautiful outcomes to unfold for yourself, as well as for the world around you. No exceptions! Moreover, hope is an expression of love in all directions. Real hope cannot be denied nor cut off from another creature. That is to say, if you cannot extend a loving hope that another's heartfelt hopes and desires are fulfilled, then I'm afraid you have no hope for yourself and therefore, no love for yourself.

To sit in the loving energy of hope or to lack it is an ongoing never-ending choice. For hope is an expression of love and we all know that life only offers us two root feelings. That is, the feeling of love and the lack thereof. All depends on the direction of your gaze… Your choices.

Now, I know these sort of moralistic calculations can sound confusing or convoluted to those whose flame of hope is nearly out. Nonetheless, all should be made aware that death is often found at the door of hopelessness. In smaller numbers, biology calls this death. But in larger numbers, biology calls this extinction.

And I say all that just to say. Providing encouragement and therefore hope to others supports the proliferation of goodness and wellbeing within the species… And that is how you say 'I love you'.

My Remarkable Adventure into Diseparabliss

My dog is a professional ball catcher. Over the years, the dog's skills continued to elevate, allowing him the extraordinary ability to catch the most difficult throws with his acrobatic maneuvers, which often made me squeal and gasp with either shock or delight. I had been wondering for quite a while why the dog loved that red ball so much, until it dawned on me that perhaps the dog is so enamored by the ball because it gives him the opportunity to leap, jump, flex, twirl and flip in ways we both never could have imagined. Thus, the ball represents an opportunity for the dog to experience the wonders of itself, its own fascinating body.

On the most ordinary hot day, I picked up my dog's favorite red ball as we raced to the park to play fetch. When we got there, I started to feel faint, then passed out. This had never happened before, maybe it was due to the intense desert climate or dehydration.

When I awakened, I saw my dog hovering over me. There was a slight pain in my head and as the pain subsided, I realized I was in an unfamiliar forest next to a stream that flowed off the edge of a cliff a thousand miles high. My gaze drifted back to my dog who was standing over me, but this time he looked different. He was clearly hungry and willing to kill for his next meal. That was the moment I could feel every cell and neuron in my body, which revealed to me that I was a small red-feathered flightless bird with legs that resembled the hindlimbs of a kangaroo. Lacking flight and the reptilian-like legs that most birds have was hardly a notice, as it quickly became overshadowed by the emotion that began to boil inside my now tiny veins... Fear!

Fearing the reality that the dog could kill me in a single bite and swallow me in just two, I ran. No! I scurried, hopped and zigzagged up and over the dense forest vegetation… Darting past trees, under fallen stumps, and around smoldering boulders. The dog, clearly in hot pursuit.

What started as fear, quickly turned into a game for the two of us. This exciting dance with death gave me the opportunity to experience my new feathered body in a way that not only tested its limits, but gave it space to perform beyond what it was supposedly designed to do. That dance with death caused every cell in my little bird-like body to nudge every molecule of DNA in an effort to deliver a message. The DNA was told by the cells: "It's time to reimagine what we thought we could do and who we thought we could become." It took feeling like a rodent to understand that the dance with death is merely fun and games. Playful as playful can be.

At the exhilarating moment the dog captures me with his bite, I immediately find myself in yet another world. Galaxies and futures away from home. Evident by the violet colored mountains that floated in the sky. Along with floating land masses that drifted slowly with the wind, appearing as islands untethered from a planet drifting overhead and in the distance. Unbeknownst to me, the islands were suspended in air by a force not too dissimilar from gravity. While clouds floated far below the floating islands, a pearly pale pink sky formed the backdrop of this sprawling realm. In this new world, I find that I have yet another body. This body feels both big and mighty, yet delicately precious.

I examine myself to discover that I am a combination of an upgraded version of a human being and an ancient god. In this body, I possess the perception, insights, and knowledge of a sorcerer. Where I come from, sorcerers like this are customarily stoned or burned at the stake, if not strangled to death. For the masses fear the power of such beings, not realizing that they too possess the same power. If only they could believe in their own greatness, which would lead them to the magic within their own consciousness. We will always silence the sorcerer. That is, until we realize that the sorcerer inside of us can no longer be held captively buried within some deep cave formed by our own denial.

Glancing around the realm, I see a similar god-like being approaching hesitantly, as if trying not to startle me. The approaching creature somehow possessing the calm of an early morning sunrise and a type of beauty only bestowed upon mermaids, so I thought. The approaching stranger begins to speak to me telepathically. Somehow, we sense each other's thoughts, intentions, emotions and desires. We proceed to engage in a wordless communication lacking in ambiguity and possessing the precision of a blade. It is impossible for secrets to exist within this kind of psychological tapestry under the physical laws of this realm.

The best way to translate our telepathic chit chat is as follows:

"Greetings my dear traveler from the great beyond. I hope you are finding comfort in your new karmic body" thought the beautiful creature possessing mermaidic beauty.

The stranger's skin is dark, speckled with small glowing spots. I look down at my body and to my surprise, I too am speckled with a unique arrangement of glowing dots. It is as if our skin is literally made out of the midnight sky from the dimension called Earth. But here, Earth feels like an impossibility, a dream whose details have already become too faint to fully recall, while also feeling so far in the past and buried deep within the wells of forgottenness.

The mermadic beauty continues "...this land is constructed by ecstasy and held together with Aww"

I pause momentarily, while inadvertently holding my breath, as I take notice that I am standing in a land where the mountains are a sparkling violet and the plant life seems to know my name. Thus, making my supposed past lives appear to be just a faint figment of my imagination. But I still feel a longing for that imaginary place I once called home. But what or where is home when you have only a muddled recollection of it?

With the elegance of a stallion, slowly batting its majestic reddish peacock feathered eyelashes, my new friend gestures for me to follow. With a bit of shyness wrapped in excitement, I take the majestic stranger's hand as I am led down a well-worn path revealing the sparkly violet sand beneath my bare feet.

The midnight dark being's thoughts continue. "As a guest in this land, let me show you around. This is the most beautiful and majestic realm of all. I hope you can sense all our tribes greeting you from afar."

I quiver as I feel the divine creature's thoughts pulse along my starry skin, followed by the overwhelming presence of tribes that I can perceive, yet not see. Thus, propelling my heart into a new understanding of life. I reply by thinking back to my new friend, turned tour guide. "It all looks and feels like the fantasy of my fantasies. Wondrous indeed."

I somehow feel my new friend laugh heartily inside, then the divine beauty thinks to me "you make it sound like you're lost."

"But truly, I've never been here nor known its existence." I assert with my thoughts.

"You say that, but I am fully aware that no visitors arrive here by accident. You have arrived in the land that only your heavens can dream of." I sense my companion's laughter erupt even harder as I am led to where the path meets a rainbow.

"I don't understand what I'm seeing…" I think to my divine friend.

"It's a rainbow. These are promised in every realm" the mermaidic beauty replies with confusion in its goddess-like eyes.

"I know that, you're so silly! But in my realm, rainbows are repelled by me. I've never managed to get this close to one... Can I touch it?" my thoughts ask for fear I could somehow be harmed or electrocuted by such an anomaly because I had forgotten, at that moment, that I too was the anomaly.

"You can do more than that. Rainbows serve as bridges for us. It will carry us to the lands that you see in the distance. Come, let me show you the Oohs and Awws of my favorite places" I sense my friend say with the enthusiasm that comes from a child when playing a game of show and tell.

The emotional thrill of zipping along rainbows causes the starry speckles of my midnight skin to glow brighter. My endearing tour guide, appearing as angelic as ever, takes me to meet many of the tribes. Tribes made up of other godess-like beings in different shapes, sizes, colors and mystical powers. Many of the tribes living amongst the pink singing trees with golden leaves. Trees that smell of harmony and whose song sounds sweet seemed to have a special song created for me. We then cross another rainbow to meet the dancing rivers that spring up into the air creating watery shapes and patterns while telling stories through their fluid formations. Here, water has the power to remain suspended in air, shape itself, and sway with a righteous exuberance.

Our playful adventure leads us to one dazzling place after another. This was clearly a place of unending adventures, wonderment and the full manifestation of [7]freedom ringing. Ringing love, joy and play. Allowing spontaneity to guide us now, we ascend to take in the view from atop the laughing mountains where the flowers run around playing hide-and-go-seek with anyone or anything willing to play… And willing I was. Unhesitatingly, I chase after and am chased by the beautifulest giggling flowers for a few rounds of play.

Seated there atop the mountain, I realize we have arrived at the fabled Mountaintop that I had previously, back in a faraway dimension, believed was just a figure of speech. My eyes capturing the mighty glare of The Promised Land in the not-so-far distance served as confirmation that I stood where I stood.

It was there that I worked up the courage to rest my hand on the warm shoulder of the goddess sitting beside me. The goddess begins to rub my back and that's when I knew the connection had always been there. The goddess pulls me closer. Like children with nowhere to go and nowhere to be, we roll around in pink blades of tall grass while the flowers played hide-and-go-seek around our bodies. The

---

[7] "Freedom ringing" pays homage to the words of the Honorable Dr. Martin Luther King's 'I Have a Dream' speech from Aug 28,1963 at the Lincoln Memorial wherein he repeatedly declares "Let freedom ring…"

flowers' play tickled our heads, shoulders, knees and toes, causing us to let out a laughter that summoned an energy that had the power to create worlds.

The goddess dares to kiss me and I dare to receive it.

The lovely goddess stands above me while I am still nestled in the grass. The mermaidic beauty appears divinely feminine in this moment and regally masculine in the next. A shift that seemed to be dictated by the guide's mood. Shaded by my guide's aroused body, I recognize this as an answered prayer as I reach up to touch the goddess. As my fingertips sense the throbbing pulses produced by my companion's regal body, it dawns on me that we have been naked throughout our entire adventure within the realm. Naked from the very moment that we had met, but I had somehow been too distracted and captivated, not solely by the beauty of this fantastical world, but also by the splendid grace and glory emanating from my masculinely feminine tour guide.

I allow my fingers to trace a few of the veins along my guide's abdomen, then allow my fingers to slide across all the warm curves and crevices that I can reach. It is clear through our continued telepathic communication that this divine beauty had desired this moment just as much as I had.

Now standing, I look into the depths of my guide's eyes as a means of taking it all in. We proceed to engage in a playfully sensuous tussle before my guide kisses me softly upon the lips.

With the passion of a storm, we exchange love grips and love thrusts. And there I am. Naked as I had been from the start, my cheek comfortably smothered in the soft grass below that smelled of sweet burnt lavender. We eventually fall into a soft cuddle, like two heat seeking cubs at the height of winter.

Life-giving vibrations flowing in, around, and through us cause our skin to transform from its starry midnight hue, to a now glowing midday blue. Both of us feeling pleasantly satiated, as we take turns filling each other's temples with a life-giving force.

As we lay there embracing one another, the glow of our bodies dim back to their starry midnight complexions. Thus causing our bodies to melt into one another. Like water mixing with water, air stirred with air. We expand to consume the everything-ness of the world around us, including the pearly sky above. Thus, our bodies form the formless sky that cradles this entire magnificent world, along with all of its contents. We proceed to sleep as the darkness of night for what was literally a few thousand eternities, but felt as timeless a daydream.

When we awaken, the pearly white skies return along with pale pink gaseous clouds and we find ourselves cuddled together back on the grass. I lift my eyes to catch my companion's warm smile. Although my guide appeared to be more masculine during our sensual roll-around, he, or dare I say she, now appears vibrantly feminine.

"My time with you has been the most incredible experience. I didn't know my homeland could feel as celestial as you have made it" I feel the angelic guide think.

"I want to be with you forever, but I feel compelled to return to wherever I came from" I reply telepathically with a guilty awareness that I could no longer remember where I came from.

"I understand and will never forget you. Let me help you get home" replies the guide, then pauses as if to honor the mood that descended upon the moment. The mood that triggered an awareness that this might be our last moment together.

"Just take this feather and squeeze it as soon as you are ready to return to the place you call home. At that moment, you will be lifted out of this realm that we call Diseparabliss. It will take you through the light speed accelerator through many more dimensions and spacetimes, then you will arrive safely into the land from which you came" the mermaidic beauty instructs while plucking a red feather from their eyelashes and delicately places it in the palm of my hand.

I stand there speechlessly thoughtless. However, my thoughts slowly return once I glance down at the gift I am handed. I am struck by the small reddish peacock feather taken from my guide that now appears to be floating in the midnight sky as it sits there against my starry skin.

"You are more brilliant than any fantasy I ever could have imagined and yet you are here. Thank you for giving me this enchanting experience" I reply with my thoughts that somehow unlock tears produced by an overwhelming sense of gratitude and sadness.

"My feelings reach past the depths for you" the mermaidic beauty proclaims.

I attempt to confess my love for the goddess before me, but I can't seem to find the telepathic thought for it. Being at a loss for thoughts, yet again. Unable to reach for nor grasp at the thoughts I desired to hold and express.

Observing my struggle, the goddess explains: "The thought or concept you are reaching for in your mind doesn't exist here."

Now feeling more confused than ever before, I wait for clarification to come from the beautiful goddess before me.

The goddess pauses briefly to take notice of the confusion expressed by my shrugged shoulders and curled toes. Then the goddess continues "...that is to say, it cannot exist alone within this realm. Here, love, joy and play cannot be divorced nor separated. They are a married trio, forming one brilliant emotion. Trees cannot thrive without their roots and leaves. Similarly, love cannot function nor operate without its defining members- joy and play. Inseparably indivisible, they are."

"How do you express that here?" I ask with a longing because this knowledge felt like freedom to my soul as I let it swirl through everything I ever was and will be.

Without warning, my guide opens their mouth to speak. Having become so accustomed to our telepathic communication, I was astonished by the simple fact that my companion had a voice.

I listen intently.

"Ogunu" the goddess announces, the sound of which rumbling the ground below our feet.

My guide repeats slowly yet deeply "Ohh-Gew-New" .

That is the moment I understood that the feeling of Ogunu is how one marries love, joy and play in holy matrimony. A holy trinity of sorts.

Now using the lips that I had only used to kiss my guide, I attempt to repeat the word as a means of tasting the magical word as it rolled off my tongue. "Ogunu" I say aloud, thus hearing my own voice for the very first time in this world.

"Will I ever see you again?" the guide asks with a sorrowful voice and melodic tone.

"Seeing you again is my deepest fantasy. But it is difficult for me to travel to Diseparabliss, seeing how I appeared here by a stroke of fate, not via a map. So, we'll have to meet somewhere in the middle. Making it a shorter journey for the two of us" I reply with a sweet tone and playful grin.

Bewildered, the guide replies "I can harness all of the magic of the galactic universes of eternity, but I've never heard of a middle ground between our two separate dimensions."

Smiling as if I had been holding a secret gift behind my back the whole time, I say "We have a magic where I come from called fantasy that I can share with you."

"I'm intrigued" the mermaidic beauty squeals.

Feeling delighted that the roles had been switched and now I get to be the teacher and show-er. I proceed to describe the magic… "When we both fantasize about being together, it is there we shall find each other."

"But how does one create a fantasy?" my guide asks pensively.

"I will start it for us." I reply.

I pause to wave my hands in the air like a conductor in sync with an orchestra. I continue by whispering "In my dreams and my fantasies and in the whispers whispered long long ago, we meet in a busy place where people are more concerned with Ogunu than they are with social norms. A place where we dance daily together, laugh endlessly together, explore new worlds and lands together. We experience different civilizations, we deepen our relationship as we navigate foreign lands and explore the great beyond."

I stare deep into my guide's eyes and continue, "we will live together, giggle together, cuddle endlessly together. In this fantasy world, we will explore new magic and realms, learn the languages of the cosmos and be a friend to nature. Using our combined wisdom and understanding of Ogunu, we create an entire universe dedicated to our loving connection."

With widened eyes, the guide replies "this is a really difficult game, it sounds so lovely, feels so real, yet seems like make-believe."

"Make-believe is where you shall find us. You just have to believe… I can already see it, squeeze it, sense it, smell it, touch it, hold it and I hope you can too" I cry.

"But I can't see what happens next" the guide admits with a trembling despair.

"You will see it as soon as you activate the fantasy inside you. Activate it now and tell me what you see. Please my dear, I need to hear what you see!" I demand, not taking no for an answer.

My guide's eyes close, as we both wait for the mind's eye to reveal the fantasy world "I see something coming into view… I see my arms wrapped around you as we stand high atop an ancient tree that bears our enormous treehouse."

The thrill of watching my goddess friend learn this new magic amuses my senses, causing me to raise my fists in the air while jumping with excitement. In so doing, I inadvertently squeeze the feather entrusted to me, which activates a series of events that I didn't know how to reverse. My body begins to elevate from the ground as a portal opens up above the canopy of trees. I slowly float up towards the gateway.

Seeing that this was our last moment, I urgently cry out once I'm just beyond my guide's reach, "Do you have a name?"

In spite of the urgency, my guide softly says, "I am your ascended reflection…"

Then I find myself even higher, nearly enveloped by the portal. From where I am now, the guide's voice is incredibly faint.

So, when the goddess shouted their last words, my ears couldn't hear it.

The angelic guide said at that last moment, in the spirit of love, joy and play, "I hope when you see the midnight sky, you will be reminded of the magic we made together… My dear, that is how we say, 'I love you' in the language of Diseparabliss."

And just like that, I awaken on my back with red ball in hand and my precious dog there beside me eager to play catch.

Oui Si Ja

If water could laugh, would it splash? If it aimed to soothe, would it flow? If it could convince us of miracles, would it make waves? If it could remind us that it will all be okay, would it present itself as tears? If it could convince us that the change we seek has already begun, would it rain down, draw in thunder and dance with lightning? If water were playful, would it spray, propel dolphins, reveal whales and provide yet another reason for kids to run, jump, giggle, and blow bubbles?

If the earth could tell us that we were mighty, would it produce mountains that provoke Aww in every direction and impregnant us with the desire to climb, explore, dream, and reach? If the earth could remind us that we are firmly supported, would it spit out trees that withstand the strongest winds and roughest storms, yet still maintain their erection and grow another season? Do the precious trees of the world cradle new hatching life to show us that flight is still possible although many may see us as weak and vulnerable?

If leaves could whisper precious secrets, would they rustle? If we needed a reason to look up, would stars sparkle, moons glow, and birds fly? If we were a part of that which creates all things, do we collectively make up the whole of that godthing? If we were a manifestation of that unseen force called Love, could we travel to the furthest edges of the earth, experience the touch of a stranger, then arrive at the mutual conclusion that we've been connected in otherworldly dimensions?

If we could be reminded that we are a part of all things seen and unseen, could we see ourselves and someone else's eye? Can we experience deep resounding connection without a shared grammatical language between us? Do our cries provoke winds, encourage hopes and unlock the doors to enlightenment?

Was there a point in our earthly history when hummingbirds were considered an absolute impossibility? Did hummingbirds get their start in fables or our wildest dreams? And has their hovering grace ever felt like a dream come to life or simply a part of an endless series of miracles?

Do starfish have a relationship to the stars above? Could we, like starfish, know all we need in order to thrive simply by knowing how we feel in relation to our surroundings? Millions of years roaming the seas and they have resisted the development of eyes. Could it be, they recognize that eyes have the power to fool, misdirect, and blind us if we're not careful? Have they resisted eyes as proof that it's not about what we see, but how far we dream. Fantaseeing and fantabeing.

Does our shared laughter build kinship? Do plants bloom in response to our loving adoration? Could your warm embrace be the stimulus that stops a war that we are both unaware of?

Does perfect love between me and you, between us and all of it, keep the earth in perfect proximity to the moon and the fireball in the sky? Awakening us to the realization that the distance between us isn't distance.

Is the darkness of night meant to remind us of the safety of the womb, the protection of our ancestral caves and of our unspoken dreams?

Are you a part of my grandest fantasy and am I yours?

Endless questions, yet they lead to one everlasting affirmative answer.

THIS IS NOT THE END

NOR IS IT THE BEGINNING

WELCOME TO THE PRESENT

Glossary

Aww- (noun, capitalized to emphasize divinity of creation) an expression triggered by experiencing the energy of creation through sight, sound, touch and/or experience

bending- (noun) relating to the notion that beginnings and endings are arbitrary points in time and space, while also being inseparable and therefore exist together as one singular event.

Diaria- (noun, feminine, capitalized) the original and true name of planet Earth given by the stars. In star language, it means: the region that blooms impossible outcomes and one day shall shine the brightest.

fantabeing- (verb) to sit in the energy and or identity of one's future/higher self, a divine act

fantaseeing- (verb) to project good into one's reality by first seeing it in the mind's eye, a type of foresight that goes beyond simple imagination and is related to clairvoyance, a divine act

fizard- (noun) fizard is created by combining fake with wizard. Referring to a judge, presiding figure, or person in authority that makes decisions that show a disregard for the ever increasing value of human life, can also be spelled as phizard which is related to phony

fizdom- (noun) fizdom is created by combining false with wizard. falsehoods or poor guidance portrayed as wisdom, can be intentional or unintentional. Oftentimes, though not exclusively, originating from individuals or groups in authority

godthing- (noun) an umbrella term that refers to concepts, all goddesses and gods. Also referring to consciousnesses and energies that have god- or goddess-like qualities

Hooraata- (noun, capitalized) the early ancestor of modern humans that were the first to walk on two feet and use language to communicate. Also refers to the original language spoken by the Hooraata

lifehunger- (noun) a hunger and/or desperation for the experience of Life, with all of its sensations, be they good or bad.

mermaidic- (adjective) possessing mermaid-like qualities either relating to essence, beauty and/or mysticism, an phenomenally exquisite beauty

Ogunu- (noun, capitalized to observe the holiness of the term) represents the inseparable holy trinity of love, joy and play

slithory- (noun) created by combining slimy with history, to depict the histories told by people and systems aiming to obscure history for political purposes by claiming which parts of history are relevant versus irrelevant.

Wonder- (noun, capitalized to emphasize divinity of creation) beautiful imaginings, also refers to the energy and/or consciousness that creates the physical world and beyond. Synonymous with Aww.

Britton Lee